HUNGRY
FOR MORE

HUNGRY
FOR MORE
ROMANTIC FANTASIES FOR WOMEN

EDITED BY
RACHEL KRAMER BUSSEL

TEMPTED
ROMANCE

Published in the United States by Tempted Romance, an imprint of
Cleis Press, Inc., 2246 Sixth Street, Berkeley, California 94710.

Printed in the United States.
Cover design: Scott Idleman/Blink
Cover photograph: Jonathan Storey/Getty Images
Text design: Frank Wiedemann

First Edition.
10 9 8 7 6 5 4 3 2 1

Trade paper ISBN: 978-1-940550-04-6
E-book ISBN: 978-1-940550-08-4

"Craig's List," by Greta Christina, was originally published in *Bending:
Dirty Kinky Stories About Pain, Power, Religion, Unicorns, & More.*

Contents

Introduction:
Getting Explicit

When we fantasize, we give ourselves space to live out the naughtiest acts we can imagine. For me, fantasizing is like taking a trip to another world, where I can be as wanton, selfish and depraved as I like—and for that matter, that's exactly what erotica writing does for me as well.

Fantasies don't follow the rules, either the ones society has set for us—and if you're a woman, our culture has plenty of sex rules to rein you in—or the ones we've set for ourselves. Anything—and everything—goes. In the twenty-one stories in this book, I've tried to include both common and unusual fantasies, ones that speak to things you might do or want to do, ones that might unnerve you, ones that touch the edges of our most cherished taboos.

The title *Hungry for More* has multiple meanings—these characters do indeed want *more*, but that doesn't necessarily mean more sex just to have more sex. Getting off isn't a numbers game to these characters; it's about accessing more pleasure, pushing more boundaries and trying new things, sometimes with new partners. Even when they get more of whatever it is they crave, they're still hungry, because fulfilling one fantasy isn't the end of their pleasure, but the beginning of a new and grand adventure.

The common thread here, whether the characters are having sex with strangers from Craig's List, the organic produce clerk or the secretary of state, is that these women are unabashed in their desires. They may recognize that others might look at them askance, as in Valerie Alexander's "Jailbait Torch Song," but they follow through anyway, not letting anyone stop them from experiencing the ultimate thrill of playing out a dirty dream that has often followed them through lovers, relationships and plenty of orgasms. These women often surprise their lovers with their adamant affirmations of lust, but they quickly realize the thrills to be found in venturing beyond their usual erotic boundaries.

The women in these pages know fantasies have a way of finding us, even—or especially—when we try to disavow them. They don't care about propriety, reputations or acceptability. These fantasies—of public sex, BDSM, strap-on play, lesbian encounters, bukkake, watching male lovers and much more—speak so loudly they cannot be ignored. They insist on being heard, seen, touched. While in real life we may keep our most treasured fantasies tucked away for our most secret selves, in these tales, women's fantasies are front and center, every explicit act laid bare. Luckily, here, in a book that perhaps you'll enjoy in bed, or the bath, or wherever you do your erotic reading, you get to watch—and live vicariously through these brazen, taboo-busting women, who are willing to go all the way in the name of living out whatever wild, wicked scenarios their lustiest selves have dreamt up. I invite you to come along for the ride.

Rachel Kramer Bussel
Red Bank, New Jersey

SUBMISSIVE

Jacqueline Applebee

I could tell you how Monty did me wrong. I could paint myself all shades of sorrowful. But that isn't in my nature, not one bit. I'm thankful for everything that happened.

I was born to serve others. I skipped a lot of school, stayed at home to help out when Ma got sick. I raised my sister's two kids when she up and ran away. Family's important to me, it don't matter what they did. I guess I'm a traditional gal when all's said and done. Either that or I'm a dumb fuck.

Kinky sex was a whole new bag for me. I found a stray book in one of the bins at work. It was a trashy romance where the heroine got hog-tied and screwed six ways to Sunday by a glamorous count. She was in her element when she was being used. But in the end, she was the one who ran the show, no matter what Count What's-His-Name thought.

When I read that book, I could almost feel a light going on in my head. I wanted some of that. I wanted to be a submissive.

So where does Monty fit into this picture? Well Mister Montgomery was something else. He was a senior partner at a law firm where I worked as a lowly cleaner. Monty was an elegant old man. He spoke like nobody else did, like he'd been educated all fancy and overseas. His suits were tailored and so fine I just wanted to reach out and touch him sometimes. He carried himself like he knew everyone was watching. For some reason, he was interested in me. Now, I polish up just fine. My clothes may not be expensive but there aren't any holes, and nothing's frayed. But most folks who worked for the firm looked right through me whenever I was around. Not that I'd see too many of them; I'd start real early and be out of there when they were still on their first fancy coffee of the day.

It was one morning when I came into work that I saw Monty. He was just coming out of his office as I trundled in.

"Gloria, I need your help." He held the door open as he pointed to his desk. "Look at it. I've tried everything, but to no avail. This is the last time I let my granddaughter meet me at the office. Do you have children, Gloria? Don't ever have children; they'll wreck your life. In fact, just don't have a family." Monty was talking a mile a minute. I wondered how much caffeine he'd had that morning.

There was a bright orange smear all over the side of his desk. From the smell I guessed it was nail varnish. But what surprised me was the fact that Monty knew my name. Most of the suits in that place would never speak to me at all.

"I think I have some acetone in my trolley."

Monty quirked an eyebrow at me. It was no big surprise he thought I was stupid. Well I may not have a law degree, but I knew my household chemicals.

Monty stood over me as I got to work cleaning the spill. He smelled good, even with the harsh odor of the acetone in the air. I started dabbing and wiping the nail varnish away. I wiggled my chest as I worked; I thought I'd give the old man an early morning thrill while nobody else was around. When I was done, I looked up at Monty. His smart trousers had a big old bulge at the front. I couldn't help but stare at it. My hand to God, it was huge!

Monty's eyes caught mine. "Ask nicely and I'll introduce you."

My mouth gaped open. I was amazed that I'd met someone just like a character in the kinky book I'd read. Monty had turned from the person I saw every morning into a complete stranger. A completely sexy stranger.

"Go on, Gloria. Beg for it."

Shit! Shit, damn and fuck it all! This guy was a piece of work. But my whole body felt like it had lit up from the inside. In the split second it took me to process what he'd said, I was already running my mouth.

"Please, Mister Montgomery, won't you let me see your dick?"

Monty laughed. "My dick?" He crouched down to my level and glared at me. "My penis is not called a dick. And you'll have to do better than that, girl." His voice was pitched so low I felt the vibrations go straight to my crotch. I was getting wet. I didn't know of another name for a dick that I felt comfortable using. Sure, my hippie grandpa used to refer to his pecker; my youngest nephew called it a wee-wee. I wasn't about to say any of those silly words.

"Please, Mister Montgomery, let me put my mouth on you. I'll make you feel real good, I swear."

Monty stood and placed a hand on my neck, angling my head so I could look at his face. "You've got five minutes to back up that claim."

He took out an honest-to-God pocket watch and tapped his foot.

Now, I've been sucking dicks for most of my adult life; I've been told I'm good at it a few times. But damn, as I unbuttoned Monty's fly, my hands were shaking like it was my first time with the boy from church behind his daddy's toolshed.

I licked at the head of his dick, burrowing down as I worked. I lifted his impressive balls from his briefs and licked them, too. My hands went behind my back as I imagined myself hog-tied, just like the heroine in my book. Monty growled when I did that. Just that one noise made my whole body flush with heat like I had a fever. I sucked him with even more enthusiasm than before. I massaged his dick with my tongue, sucking and pressing with my mouth and lips. I knew he was coming when his smooth rocking motions started getting rough and crazy. He came inside me. I felt so proud, I couldn't stand it. Here was someone who appreciated my skills, who wanted what I had to offer. It was like a dream. That is, it was like a dream until Monty pulled out of my mouth abruptly.

"Time's up." He wiped at the tip of his cock and held out his sticky fingers. I didn't know if he wanted me to clean his hand with my polishing cloth or lick it clean with my tongue. It didn't matter. I'd made a fantasy come true. I felt like a submissive.

Monty was in the office real early every day after that. Sometimes he brought in a pair of handcuffs and locked me to the filing cabinet. I asked him if he could hog-tie me, but he told me I didn't get to choose the toys. Toys? This wasn't a game for me. I longed to feel helpless and wanton and be desirable at the same time. I wanted flowing gowns and Victorian castles. I wanted a little romance to make me feel like a true submissive. But Monty laughed when I told him that.

"We are not equals, Gloria, not in this room or out of it."
He patted me on the head like I was some kind of stray dog.
"Don't get ideas above your station. It will only lead to disap-
pointment." I hated the sound of his voice.

"So what we do every morning, it don't mean a thing to
you?" My voice was quiet, like even I didn't want to hear the
question.

Monty shrugged. Even that movement was elegant. "You're
an interesting diversion. But I don't associate myself publicly
with the hired help."

I looked at him defiantly, rattling my cuffed hands against
the filing cabinet. "This feels pretty associated to me."

Monty's face broke into a scowl. He unlocked me from the
heavy cuffs. "The microwave in the kitchen is stained inside
and out. Please ensure it is spotless before the others arrive."

I heard him loud and clear. I got up and left.

I trudged home later that day, thinking about what Monty
had said. Did all dominants think of their subs as disposable?
Was I nothing but an expendable mouth to be fucked? I'd
briefly thought I had something of a connection with Monty,
but I guess I should have known better. He was just like every
other man I'd ever known. Submission wasn't the same as
abuse or neglect, I was sure of it. Monty was a god-awful
dominant. Some part of me knew they all couldn't be that
way. But I was still going to burn that damn book as soon as
I got home.

I stopped believing in luck an awful long time ago, but as I
sat waiting for my bus to arrive, I looked down to see a colorful
flyer curled up on the side of the road. Just a few letters were
visible, but they came into focus as I spelled them out in my

head: *S-U-B*. I picked up the flyer and stuffed it in my pocket. I waited until I got home before I scooted to the bathroom to read it. If it was a voucher for half-price sandwiches, I'd feel all kinds of foolish. But to my relief, it was for a club night happening the coming Saturday, called *Submissives Under the Bridge*. I was going to that club if it was the last thing I did.

Saturday saw me standing outside of an old building under a railroad bridge on the edge of town. I paid my entrance fee to a burly man at the front desk, counting the bills carefully. The whole building rattled as a train passed by on the elevated tracks.

"There's a changing room at the side," the man said, pointing in a vague direction.

I was wearing my smartest dress. I wasn't about to change it for anything else. But then I saw what some of the folks inside were wearing and I understood what he'd meant. I spent a good ten minutes just wandering around with a slack mouth, gazing at the pretty outfits everyone wore. I saw corsets and top hats, rubber and lace and so much bare skin. It was better than Christmas and Halloween all rolled into one.

I made my way over to a large glass cage set into a wall. A young man lay inside. He was completely naked. I moved closer, trying not to be too obvious. I thought the little thing was asleep. His eyes were closed, so I could see that his long brown lashes were pretty and delicate. He had a smile on his face, a contented expression like he didn't have a care in the world. But then his eyes fluttered open, all brown and deep and sweet like molasses. He saw me. His smile grew wide. I smiled back, and it was then that I felt something warm and light start to glow inside me once more.

I would have spent longer admiring the man, but two women

rushed up to the cage and started tapping on the glass. His attention went elsewhere.

The music in the club was loud. The drinks were expensive. But there was so much to enjoy despite all of that. I watched a woman tie a rope dress around a big gal with tiny nipples. I was almost hypnotized as two men stroked long feathers across each other's chest. I flinched as a bald black man whipped a figure pressed up against a wooden frame. Each crack of the whip sounded like a gunshot; it made me feel nervous as hell.

I sat in a quiet corner as the clubbers continued to enjoy themselves. My luck continued to be good, as the naked boy from the cage sauntered toward me.

"Mind if I sit?" He pointed to the space next to me on the low couch.

I nodded as he laid a towel on the seat and then placed himself down. I took the opportunity to glance over at him, taking in all the delicious details I'd missed earlier. He had tanned skin with not a single tan line. The thought of him out in the sun, completely nude, made me swallow hard.

I'm sure he knew I was looking for longer than I should. He leaned over. "I'm Jeremy." He shook my hand.

"Gloria."

"Wanna drink?"

"Sure. Just a Coke," I replied, and then I wondered where he kept his money. "You don't have to," I said quickly, but he was off, scampering away like a cute puppy. Thankfully Jeremy must have had a tab, because I didn't see him fishing a twenty out of his ass or anything like that. He gave me my drink with another smile that lit up the room.

"So you like being naked, Jeremy?" I asked, genuinely curious.

The boy stretched out, showing me all of his good stuff in the process. "It's natural. It's comfortable. And it's seriously sexy."

I liked this straight-talking boy. "What's the deal with the cage?"

"I like to be admired and petted."

"Like a dog?"

"More like an exotic lizard out in the sun." He held out an arm. "Feel how smooth I am."

I ran a finger up and down his arm; he wasn't lying about being smooth. It was then that I noticed he didn't have much in the way of hair anywhere on his body. There was some soft fuzz on his head, and his lashes were long, but that was it.

"I bet I could slide right off you," I joked. "And I've never petted a lizard before, but I've admired plenty of them."

Jeremy's eyes were stupidly soft as he looked over at me. "Why not give me a go?"

I held my arms open. Jeremy crawled into my lap.

"Such a good pet, aren't you?" I crooned. I honestly didn't know where these words came from, but my new friend sighed with pleasure as I spoke, so I knew it was a good thing. My hands stroked over his thighs. "You're pretty. Can I touch you some more?" I guess pets don't have much need for talking, because Jeremy just opened his legs wider for me. His cock was small, but growing in size as he got hard. I didn't have any fancy equipment on me, like the characters in the kinky book, but right then I didn't care. I stroked my nails down his dick, gentle at first and then with more force. Jeremy hissed with what sounded like pain.

"Did I hurt my pet?" I whispered.

Jeremy nodded, but he grinned and then kissed me on the cheek. "Do it again?"

"Okay, but you've gotta tell me if it's too much. Can you do that?"

Jeremy smiled at me, but remained silent.

I grasped his dick in my firm hand. "I asked you a question."

Jeremy's eyes went saucer wide. He arched up in my lap. "Yes, Gloria."

The warm feeling inside me turned white hot. A wave of contentment washed over me like I'd taken a hit from my hippie grandpa's bong. I was instantly addicted to my new friend.

You know what the strangest part of this was? It wasn't giving a hand job to a naked boy who thought himself a pet. It wasn't that we were doing this in public either. The strangest thing was the way I felt so at ease with it all. All the times I'd buried my nose in my kinky book, I'd never once fantasized about being in the dominant role. I never thought I'd be the one to take charge. Which was plain dumb as taking care of someone was second nature to me. Hell, I'd been looking after folks all of my life. Why stop now?

Jeremy screwed up his eyes. His whole body trembled when he came in my hand. And then he wrapped his arms around me, squeezing me, murmuring crazy, happy words in my ear.

"You did good, little pet." I kissed him on the forehead. "But you made me all sticky and messy."

"Sorry," he whispered. "Washroom's over there." He led me to the shared facilities. I thought he'd follow me inside, but when I turned around he was gone. I sighed to myself, my shoulders suddenly heavy. He'd had his fun, and then he'd split. Just like every man I knew.

The night was a bust. Sure it was interesting to see so many folks having fun, but I was about ready to give up on the whole dominance and submission thing. There didn't seem to be any space for someone like me in this scene. I just didn't fit.

I dried my hands and adjusted my dress. When I opened the bathroom door, Jeremy was standing there. He had two naked people, one a man and one a woman, on either side.

"Gloria, meet my little tribe."

I was full to bursting with relief. "There are more of you?"

"Abby and Marco, meet Gloria. She's the best."

The other members of the naked tribe all started squealing and chattering with excitement. Everyone wanted a hug from me. Everyone wanted to play with me. They jostled me off to a semiprivate room.

Marco snuggled in my lap. "I chewed up the paper this morning, Gloria. Can you punish me for it?" He held up a worn slipper. Marco had twinkling blue eyes and a naughty smile. I was at a loss for words, which was a first for me.

Abby sat at my feet. "I've been supergood today. I need rewarding." She looked up at me with hopeful brown eyes. "I'm a demanding pet, but you'll get used to me." She flashed me a toothy smile.

"And what will I get for so much hard work?" I asked.

All three of my submissive friends grinned at me. They pushed me back on the cushions, and then kisses and touches started coming my way. Marco and Jeremy helped me take off my dress and my bra. They both sucked on my tits like there was no tomorrow. Abby went south, nipping at my thighs until she worked her way to my crotch. I looked down to see her head disappear between my legs. I didn't need to see what she was doing with her mouth to know how good it felt. These little creatures were turning me into a new person with every swipe of their tongues on my skin. They didn't stop until I'd had an orgasm so powerful, my voice damn near broke. They all hugged me afterward in a big sticky, happy mess.

That night was the start of something truly special for me and all my little ones. Jeremy called me a Service Top much later, but back then I just called myself happy.

You see, I could tell you that Monty did me wrong. I could tell you that he was just another useless, domineering man who made me feel like shit. But what he did only drove me to my new family, my new tribe. He showed me how not to behave with a submissive in my care. I've got the proof right here in my arms that I treat my little ones right. They all love me for it. And that's all that matters to me.

HAPPY ENDINGS

Giselle Renarde

It's kind of weird how this all came about. My assistant, Maya, asked for the afternoon off so she could participate in a documentary film. When I asked what it was about, she said *happy endings.*

I didn't know what she meant, but Maya seemed awfully embarrassed. "When I was nineteen I worked as a masseuse. It wasn't on my résumé because…well, I knew what people would think."

I still didn't know what she was talking about, but I didn't ask a second time.

"Anyway, a girl I used to work with is making a documentary about happy endings. I would never give them. I thought it was gross. She wants to interview me on the con side. She's got enough girls who are pro."

"Yes, of course," I said. "Go ahead. Should be a very interesting film."

Maya grinned and called out, "Thanks, Linda," as she skipped from my office.

Happy endings? Call me naïve, but I honestly had no clue what she meant. Thank goodness for Google!

I must admit, I was a little shocked after reading the definition: *A happy ending massage culminates in sexual contact, usually manual or oral stimulation. Men are typically clients for these offerings, but some women also request happy endings. This activity is illegal in America and not performed at legitimate spas.*

What kind of a place had Maya worked, if her fellow masseuses were prostituting themselves to clients? My stomach turned, thinking about sweet Maya faced with rampant erections, and men begging her to provide some relief.

At least, that was my initial impression.

As the days passed, I started looking at Maya differently. I would spot her at the coffeemaker, or bent over the photocopier, and imagine those tiny hands working a stranger's oily flesh. In the beginning, I pictured her massaging fat old men, then slimmer, younger men, and then...me.

It got to the point where I could barely breathe when she entered my office. She would say, "Linda, are you okay? Your cheeks are all red."

"I'm fine," I would tell her. "Hot flashes. Just you wait!"

She'd laugh and fetch me a glass of water. It was more than I could stand. I hadn't felt intimate touch since my cheating bastard of an ex-husband ran off with a close friend of ours. When he left me, my body shut down. I didn't want another man. I didn't want anyone, not even myself.

And suddenly, there was Maya, making me throb, making me wet. God, I wanted her to touch me, but I couldn't ask. Just couldn't. Above all else, I was a professional woman, and responsible VPs resist the temptation to seduce their staffers. I'd always believed that, and one little all-consuming crush wasn't going to sway me.

But I needed *something*. I started touching myself in the shower, but I never really got anywhere. My pussy would ache all day, and I couldn't seem to satisfy it. After a while, my brain felt like it was on fire. I became so irritated with myself that I started scratching at work, leaving red claw marks down my neck and my chest. Maya said I should see a doctor.

One day, on a whim, I asked, "How is that documentary coming along?"

She gave me a very strange look. "Weird that you'd ask. It's premiering at a little film festival next Friday. Want to come?"

"No, no." *Yes, yes!* "I don't want to cramp your style. It'll be all young people, I'm sure."

"Linda, don't say stuff like that." Maya shook her head. "Anyway, my friend wants me to invite everyone I know. She's afraid no one will show up."

"Okay," I said before Maya could change her mind. "I'll be there."

And I was there, with bells on. Okay, not bells, but my best black dress over my most slimming undergarments. I sat on my own while Maya joined her incredibly attractive young friends. The film was truly eye-opening for me.

One woman in particular made me sit up and take notice. Her name was Shari, and she was on the pro side of the happy endings issue. "Massage represents release and relief. It's an intimate interaction, and it kicks up arousal in a lot of people. I think the natural progression is a happy ending. Touch and sexuality are so intricately interwoven. I don't want my clients leaving frustrated."

That made so much sense. Why was it okay for a masseuse

to rub your back but not your front? The divide started to seem arbitrary.

After the film, there was a reception in the lobby. I'd lost track of Maya, but I spotted Shari, the eloquent advocate of happy endings. My god, was she tall! Her red velvet gown clung to her firm breasts while a black shawl draped haphazardly over her shoulders. I felt starstruck, seeing her there. My feet just started moving, and they didn't stop until I was standing right in front of her.

"Can I make an appointment?"

That's what I said. No small talk. Straight to the chase.

"Sure." As she slipped her phone from her purse, she introduced herself.

"I know," I said. "I saw you in the film."

I stared into her dungeon-dark eyes, hoping she'd know what I wanted—hoping I wouldn't have to tell her. She must have understood, because she smiled mysteriously as she looked up from her phone. "Are you busy now?"

"Now? What, you mean like right now?" I stammered like an idiot. "No, I'm free. Now is perfect."

If I'd put it off or scheduled the massage for another day, I'd surely have lost my nerve.

We slipped into a taxi and chatted about the movie. I didn't even know what I was saying, I was so lost in the enormity of paying for sex. Really, that's what I was about to do.

As Shari unlocked the door of an unlit spa, she said, "We closed up for the night so everyone on staff could go to the film premiere. It'll be just the two of us."

"Oh, good."

My stomach roiled as Shari led me up a narrow staircase. I don't know what I was expecting. I just wanted it not to be sleazy. Luckily, when she opened the door at the top of the stairs, the setting sat somewhere between comfortable and clinical. I could handle that.

There was a massage table in her little room, and a fountain, some bamboo shoots, other greenery. Shari left the room while I undressed fully. I bristled with an anxious, almost embarrassed sort of heat. She knocked before coming back in the room, and by then I was flat on the prepared table, with my face through that odd pillow with the hole in the middle.

Shari gave me a whole lot of information, but my ears were buzzing. I had no idea what she said. When she set her oiled hands on my skin, I melted. It had been so long. She wouldn't have believed me if I'd told her. *Years.* So many years since I'd been touched—even like this, just her hands on my back. Without warning, I started crying.

At first, I kept it quiet. I didn't want her to hear me whimpering, but when the full-on sobs took over, I couldn't hide my sorry state. Shari asked if I'd like a tissue, and when I arched up I caught my first glimpse of her. She'd taken off her gown. What she wore now was black, like a corset with panties. She reminded me of a flamenco dancer, for some reason. She seemed wildly passionate, but totally in control.

"Thanks." I dabbed my eyes, then blew my nose. "I'm sorry about this. I don't know what's gotten into me."

"It's very common," she said. "Massage releases pent-up emotions. No need to feel sorry."

When I settled back in, with my tissues balled up in my fist, she asked if I'd like her to work her way up from my calves. Yes, I wanted that. Very much so. When her warm palms traced oil up my legs, I melted all over again. I'd never thought of my calves as sensitive, but when Shari touched them, raw energy swirled through my pelvis. That sensation—I recognized it from years ago. From when I was a teenager, when I was in college. Long, long ago.

"That feels amazing," I said. My head was spinning, and so was my belly. My whole body felt dizzy.

Standing to one side, Shari worked her way up my thighs. The closer she got to my naked rear, the more intensely that warm energy swirled between my legs. I stared down at the floor, smiling like an idiot, and picturing Shari in her black lingerie. When she started kneading my asscheeks, I actually groaned.

"Sorry," I said, feeling dreadfully embarrassed.

"Don't be." Her smile gleamed in her voice. "Make all the noise you like."

I wasn't shy after that. In truth, I couldn't keep it in. When she stroked my ass with scented oil, I moaned like a monster. In my entire life, I don't think anyone had ever touched me in quite that way. It felt amazing.

After a while, Shari asked, "Are you ready to flip?"

I didn't even answer her—I just did it. I turned over on the massage table and opened my legs. Before I could stop myself, I ended up asking, "Do you ever massage people naked?"

Her lips pursed beautifully, and then she smiled. "Only if I really like them."

She must have really liked me, because she unstrung her corset and slipped out of it right before my eyes. Her body made mine pulse. I wanted to spread oil across her golden skin. Her firm breasts pointed in my direction as I stared at her bare pussy. I wished I'd shaved mine, too. I could just imagine her palm pressing against my baby-smooth cunt.

Instead, she ran her fingers through the dark curls between

my legs. When I felt her slick hand against the pulpy, pounding mass of my clit, my whole body melted into the vinyl cushion. "Oh, that's good. That's sooo good."

She rubbed my pussy with the meat of her palm. I don't know if it was the oil or Shari's nudity, or just the fact that I hadn't been touched intimately in almost a decade, but my sleeping body woke up. My pussy gushed as I pressed it against her hand. She wasn't doing anything special, not that I could see, but I didn't need much convincing.

"Want me to go in?" she asked.

Her breasts surged as she rubbed me, like her whole body was doing the work. I stared at them as I tried to unpack her question. "Go in?"

She held up two fingers and raised an eyebrow.

"Oh!" When did I become such a naïve old woman? "Yes, okay."

Shari doused my mound with oil, and just feeling that warm, slick stuff sliding over my hot folds made me moan. When she pressed two fingers into my pussy, my bones turned to pudding. She moved slowly inside of me, looking for something...and finding it.

"Oh my god!" I arched on the table. "What is that?"

"Feels good, huh?" She rubbed that strange place somewhere inside me, and I wondered if that could possibly be my G-spot. If it was...well, I finally understood what all the fuss was about.

"Thank you," I said, almost in a whisper.

Shari stroked me with her fingers, tracing gentle circles around my clit. She obviously knew what she was doing. My swollen lips felt fatter by the second. She summoned the juice that had been hibernating inside of me forever. At least, it felt like forever since I'd been aroused like this, and unashamedly so.

"Don't stop," I said, gripping Shari's wrist. From the look she gave me, I thought maybe I shouldn't have done that, but she didn't say anything, so I didn't let go. And then she jumped and laughed and I asked, "What?"

"Didn't you feel that?" She rubbed me faster, inside and out. "Your pussy's milking my fingers. You must really like this."

My eyes fluttered. "I really do."

I didn't speak after that, not in words. I surrendered to the sensations Shari aroused in my body. It wasn't just one sensation—oh no. She made me want to push, and she made me want to pull. I bucked at her hand, launching my hips up in the air and then right back down. I wasn't in control of my actions anymore. My thighs tensed. I held my legs stiff as she scoured my clit. Then she tickled my G-spot and I nearly flipped off the table. She had to hurl her naked self on my belly to keep me in place.

"Mmm!" I shrieked and shouted, keeping my lips pressed shut. "Mmm-mm-mmm!"

My arms thrashed, and Shari jammed her tight breasts into my skin. I thrust my hips, forcing her to writhe on top of me. My brain had set itself on fire. I couldn't think. All I knew was my want—more, more, more!

The pulpy ache of my pussy expanded to devour my belly and my breasts. My eternally soft nipples drew into tight, dark buds. I reached for my breasts, cupping them, squeezing them, and that threw me well over the edge.

I wailed as the pleasure morphed into pain. Suddenly, my pussy felt huge, like a balloon set to explode. I cried, "Stop! Please! Enough!"

Shari rose from my body like a mist, withdrawing her fingers from my pussy and wiping them with a cloth. I couldn't catch my breath. My chest rose and fell. The whole room seemed hazy, like it was lost in a fog.

When Shari leaned across my thigh and blew on my clit, I shivered and laughed. It took a while to find my words, but when I did, I gushed. I must have thanked her a million times, and told her how glad I was that she'd brought me here, how grateful, how long it had been. I guaranteed that I'd make ours a standing appointment. I would come back every week—twice a week, if she'd have me.

When I ran out of breath and finally stopped talking, Shari said, "I'm glad you enjoyed it. To tell you the truth, women very rarely walk through that door. I've never given a full release massage to another woman."

She seemed like such an expert, like she knew exactly what to do. I said, "I don't believe it. You did such a fabulous job. I know I'm naïve, but there's no way that was your first time."

"Well…" Shari cocked her head coquettishly. "My first time at work."

CRAIG'S LIST

Greta Christina

On her twenty-fourth birthday, she decided there were three things she wanted to do before she turned twenty-five. Sexual things. All three involved taking stupid risks, putting her body into the hands of people she knew nothing about and had no reason to trust. All three involved Craig's List.

She knew she had to do them now. The older she got, the less reckless she'd become. She knew that if she waited until she was thirty, she wouldn't be brave enough, or stupid enough, to try this. And she knew she'd always regret it if she didn't try.

The first one she called Craig's List Roulette. She would go to the Casual Encounters ads, the Men Seeking Women section. She would pick an ad at random. No matter what it said, she would answer it. Unless she was literally and physically unable to comply with the ad's request, she would answer it.

She would use a random number generator, so she couldn't cheat.

She knew how stupid this was, how reckless, how dangerous. But she didn't want to be just another boring horny slut playing the personals. She wanted to set a new standard for sluts. She wanted to be the slut by which all other sluts measured themselves. Besides, reckless and dangerous was kind of the point. She wanted a real adventure—and in a real adventure, you weren't in control.

The ad headline read, *Young, horny, need to get sucked.* Perfect. Simple. Easy to take care of. She took a picture of herself, naked on her knees, and sent it with her reply.

She was at his dorm in twenty minutes. He wasn't as cute as she'd hoped—she thought he might have used a fake picture, actually—but that was okay. Weirdly, it was part of the charm. She closed his dorm-room door behind them, and dropped to her knees, thinking with a hard thump in her clit of how she had been manipulated, how she was being used. She dropped her head back and opened her mouth. He unzipped and pushed himself into her, and she opened wide and let him fuck her mouth.

He kicked her out politely when he was done, and she went home and masturbated for an hour and a half. She masturbated on her knees, with a dildo in her mouth and a vibrator between her legs. She kept thinking she couldn't possibly come any more...and then she would remember what she had just done, and her sore, tired clit would throb again, demanding just one more.

She was back on Craig's List the next day.

She hadn't expected that. When she first decided to do her three adventures, she'd assumed that she'd play each of them just once. But she loved Craig's List Roulette. It was like slut boot camp. It was like an accelerated study program in human sexuality. It was like a multi-week intensive course in letting go. Her requirements got a little more restrictive—the guy had to ask for something specific, he couldn't ask to do drugs together, he couldn't ask to do it more than once—but she stuck to the spirit of the game with remarkable discipline.

She landed on *Wanna watch me play with myself?* and was soon in a home-built weight room in a dingy garage, watching an oiled-up bodybuilder straddle his weight bench and stroke his cock, repeatedly murmuring, "You like what you see?", his eyes never leaving her face. She landed on *Anyone for a car date right now?* and found herself fumbling in the back of a Camry with a married ad exec, his hands groping at her tits, his cock pushing against her crotch through her panties, his breath pungent with weed. She landed on *Oral from behind* and an hour later was on her knees in a cheesy bachelor pad in the suburbs, a noisy tongue slurping at her pussy and occasionally, hesitatingly, perhaps even guiltily, slipping into her asshole. She landed on *Offering $$$ for pussy licking,* and thought, *Sure, why not?* and then was on her back in a hotel bed with a tongue between her legs and three twenties on the bedside table. She thought she'd feel different after, and was surprised when she didn't.

She landed on *Just give me a blow job* and *Can a guy get a blow job please?* and *Looking for a woman in need of a facial* with perverse excitement. She loved how openly selfish they were. She loved how slutty it made her feel, how sordid, to get on her knees and open her mouth to a man who expressed no interest whatsoever in what she might need or want. She loved how it made her feel both purely sexual and purely invisible. And she loved feeling like the only woman in the city who would ever answer their ad. It made her feel extreme. Hard core. Special.

She landed on *Looking for a woman to spank,* and thought,

About fucking time. That was the first one—and the last—where she laid out her own guidelines. "I've never done this before," she told the guy. "I really want to. I want this to go well." The gentleman was older: in his early sixties, a little soft, a little frail, but patient and careful and grateful. He told her that she was beautiful, that she was bad, that he was going to teach her a lesson, that he was going to take care of her. He spanked her gently, until she wanted more than anything for him to spank her harder; and he spanked her harder, until she had no idea what she wanted anymore. He was the first one—and the only one—that she wished she could go back to. But that wasn't how the game was played.

She always felt a little guilty about the ones who just wanted to service her; the ones who ate her pussy or licked her feet or gave her long, drawn-out massages. It seemed like missing the point. But then she'd remember: this was what they'd asked for. When she lay back and let herself be taken care of, she was giving them the service they wanted more than anything.

It was disappointing sometimes. Naturally. There were clumsy men, smelly men, liars. But she kept the game up, a bit longer perhaps than she would have...because she was putting off the second one. She was a little afraid of the second one.

The second game, she called Motel Slut. It took a little more courage, more aggressiveness, since she had to place her own ad. Casual Encounters, Women Seeking Men. The ad read:

I am in the Star Motel on Broadway. I am in Room 314. I am naked. I will fuck the first man who shows up, in any position you like. Just tell me what you want, and don't talk about anything else. If the Do Not Disturb sign is up, you're too late—someone else got here first.

She placed the ad from her laptop in the motel room. The first man showed up in ten minutes. He was out of breath from running up the stairs. She hung the Do Not Disturb sign on the door, and immediately took off her robe. She was naked, as promised. "Tell me how you want to do it."

The man was goggle-eyed. "Can we do it doggie style?"

"Don't ask. Just tell."

He didn't seem to understand. But he went along. "Okay. Let's do it doggie style."

She gestured to the lube and condoms on the nightstand, and got on her hands and knees on the bed.

She played the image in her head again and again as he unzipped his pants and crawled between her knees. Opening the motel door to the stranger. Dropping her robe to show him her naked body. Saying nothing but a few terse words about sex. Putting herself silently on her hands and knees on the motel bed, and opening her legs so he could fuck her. She played the image again and again, as he pushed himself inside her. It was like a feedback loop screaming into her cunt. He wasn't a great lover—crude, a little clumsy—but it didn't matter. She felt like a character in a porno movie. She dropped into the feeling like a stone dropping into the sea.

Like Craig's List Roulette, she hadn't planned on doing this more than once. And like Craig's List Roulette, she was hooked after the first time. The next day, she did it again. She opened the motel door for another stranger; she dropped her robe; she lay on her back and spread her legs when he told her to; she let herself get fucked. And when he left, she took the Do Not Disturb sign off the door, and waited for the next one.

She did three guys that day. Seven the next. After that, she slowed down a bit: kept it to once a week, and usually no more than three or four in a day.

Some of them were simple. They just wanted a girl on her back with her legs open. And that was fine. It had a certain primal, meat-puppet charm. Some were more imaginative. And that was better. She liked being told to sit on the guy's dick and face away from him. To straddle him on a chair like a stripper and give him a lap dance that turned into a fuck. To lie back on the cheap motel desk, her butt scooted all the way to the end, her fingers spreading her cunt apart, her face turned to the wall. She liked being told to lie facedown on the bathroom floor, her tits getting scraped by the cold tile as she got fucked from behind.

Sometimes it was hard. One of them told her, "I want to fuck you in the ass." She'd never done that before. Somehow, by a statistical freak, it had never come up in Craig's List Roulette. But the habit of compliance had become strong, and it didn't occur to her to say no. She gestured to the lube and the condoms on the nightstand, and said only, "Slowly, please. I've never done this before." And she got on her hands and knees on the bed.

It hurt a little. He wasn't as slow as he should have been. But that was kind of okay. Again, she pictured where she was, what she had done to get here, what she was doing now. She remembered that she was being fucked in the ass for the first time, in a sleazy motel room by a man she'd never met: a man she'd undressed for and offered herself to the moment he walked in the room. She remembered that she was facedown on the bed and that her ass was being pushed open, too fast and too hard, because she'd invited any man who showed up at her door to fuck her any way he wanted. She remembered what a slut she was, that she'd asked for this, that she deserved this. She buried her face in the bed and whimpered: a genuine cry of pain and fear, blending imperceptibly with a moan of abandon.

She'd pictured her first time getting fucked in the ass a hundred times. She'd never pictured it happening like this. It was a hundred times better than she'd ever imagined.

She loved Motel Slut. And again, she kept the game up longer than she would have...because she was putting off the third one. She was more than a little afraid of the third one.

The third game, she called Pick the First.

It required a lot of courage. She was glad she'd put herself through Slut Boot Camp first. And it required strict honesty with herself. She couldn't rely on the randomness of a number generator, or the randomness of which man happened to be reading Craig's List at the moment she placed her ad.

In Pick the First, she had to read the ads on Craig's List. Casual Encounters, Men Seeking Women. She had to pick the first ad that turned her on; the first ad that made her want to masturbate. And she had to send him this email. She wrote it ahead of time, before she started looking, so she couldn't cheat.

I don't want to negotiate. I just want to do what you tell me. Please tell me what you want me to do, and what you want to do to me. Please tell me everything you can think of, now, so we don't ever have to talk about it again. If what you want is okay, I'll be at the Java Jive Cafe on 4th Street this Saturday at noon, with a black carnation in my hair. Please meet me there, and then take over.

It took longer than she'd thought to find the right ad. She considered *Submissive women needed for thick cock,* but the poorly lit photos of his torso and cock made her flinch with distaste. She thought about *Arrive, bend over, submit, leave,* but the scene he laid out stopped at sex and went nowhere interesting. She regretfully passed on *Cruel, humiliating, abusive and sadistic*: the headline made her clit jump like a kangaroo, but the ad was a letdown, with no juicy details, and an equivocating manner that put the lie to the promise of the headline. She kept an eye out for her spanking friend, but he wasn't on Craig's List that day. She saw *Brutal M seeks submissive W,* and opened it. It read:

I am a hard and unyielding man seeking a woman to whom I can do things. The things I want to do are not nice. I will want to use you sexually, humiliate you, hurt you, make you helpless. I will want you frightened, and suffering, and willing and compliant throughout. Am not looking for either brats or doormats. You should have desires, so I can deny them. You should have spirit, so I can break it.

It made her uneasy. To say the least. But it was the one she kept coming back to. The one she knew she'd be jerking off to. So bolstered by weeks of rigorous self-training in impulsive carelessness, she copied and pasted her pre-written reply, and hit *Send.*

He replied with a torrent of obscenity.

Implements he was going to use to beat her ass until she cried. Objects he was going to insert into her. Degrading positions he was going to force her into. Other men he was going to lend her to. He said he was going to wrestle her onto her back, pin her arms to the bed with his knees, and force his cock down her throat until she gagged. He said he was going to tie her hands so she couldn't fight, gag her so she couldn't scream, tie her legs apart, and whip her pussy before he fucked it. And then he was going to do the same to her asshole.

He said he was going to punish her righteously and ruthlessly for serious offenses. That he was going to punish her cruelly and unjustly for trumped-up offenses. That he was going to punish her for no reason at all except that he felt like it. He said he was going to make her spread her asshole apart for him with her hands, make her beg him to punish her by putting things inside it, make her apologize tearfully for being a bad girl while he did it. He said he was going to slap her face and call her a filthy whore while she sucked his cock.

He said he was going to rape her.

He went on for three pages. He apparently took *tell me everything you can think of* seriously. He finished with the words:

None of this is up for discussion. You will comply with all of it. You may show reluctance—I like reluctance—but you may not show resistance. Except when I rape you. When I rape you, I expect you to resist. I will see you on Saturday.

He scared the crap out of her.

She knew this was a bad idea. Even with all her other Craig's List adventures, she hadn't done a third of the things he was talking about. She knew she was in over her head with this one. But she'd known that Craig's List Roulette and Motel Slut had been bad ideas, too. And they had been the best bad ideas of her life.

She put the date in her calendar for Saturday. And cleared the rest of her calendar.

BRINGING THE HEAT

Tiffany Reisz

Strike one was the game itself.

By the fifth inning, Jada decided her first date with Ryan would be her last date with Ryan. This wasn't even a date. It was a minor league baseball game in ninety-eight-degree weather. In other words, torture.

"Hey, wanna go get us some drinks?" Ryan asked, handing her his credit card. He stood next to her—and had been standing next to her for the entire hour. At first she thought he did it to shield her from the blistering sun. But no, he just wanted to see the action better.

"You're buying. How chivalrous." Jada forced the sarcasm from her voice and stopped herself from rolling her eyes. Her mother taught her better than that. Then again her mother never went on a date with Ryan.

"I take care of my girl."

My girl? This was the first date and he called her "my girl"?

Ryan looked down and winked at her over his sunglasses.

Strike two.

She would never ever have sex with this man.

Ever.

Jada hauled herself to her feet. Sticky with sweat, she left half her thighs on the seat.

"Wait." Ryan grabbed her arm. "You don't want to miss this."

"What?" she asked. "I told you I don't know anything about baseball."

"Flak Gordon's up to bat. Just watch."

"Don't you mean Flash Gordon?"

"No, Baby. Flak. Real name is Jack but Flak's his nickname. You're about to see why."

She exhaled heavily as she raised her hand to shield her eyes.

"What am I watching?"

"Martyrdom." Ryan grinned broadly, saying the word with relish.

"What?"

"Pay attention," Ryan said in a rude and testy tone.

Jada ignored the tone and watched. The player in question—Flak Gordon, number 29 batting for the Devils—walked to home plate with a loose easy stride. A handsome boy, he couldn't have been more than twenty-three or twenty-four. He had an all-American look to him. Their seats were close enough she could see the grin on his face. Why was he smiling?

The pitcher wound up and threw the ball. Flak swung and missed. He didn't swing at the second pitch. On the third pitch, the entire crowd groaned as the ball hit him in the shoulder.

"What the hell?" Jada asked as Flak threw his bat down and jogged to first base.

"They need to load the bases," Ryan explained. "Leaning into the pitch and getting hit with the ball is a surefire way to get on first."

"Damn. That must have hurt." Jada couldn't even see the ball it traveled so fast.

"The pitchers bring the heat when Flak comes up to bat," said a man in front of them, eager to join in her baseball education. "He doesn't seem to mind. Must be a masochist."

Masochist? Suddenly this game started to get interesting.

Flak hit first base and some guy wearing the same uniform patted him on the back. The back pat didn't stay a back pat, however.

"Is that guy rubbing Flak's ass?" she asked Ryan.

"He's the first base coach."

"Looks more like he's trying for third base to me."

"Don't make this a gay thing." Ryan glared at her.

"What? You don't think there are gay baseball players?" She sure as hell hoped there were gay baseball players. She loved the thought of two guys having sex, manly guys, guys other straight guys wanted to be like. One of her favorite nighttime masturbation fantasies was watching two men together. Two cocks were always better than one.

"Don't be gross."

"Gay men aren't gross."

"Aren't you getting us drinks?"

"Get your own." She threw the credit card at his feet and walked out of the stands. She wouldn't have minded a baseball game on the third date or fourth date. She wouldn't have minded going with him as a favor. But Ryan had been pursuing her at work for weeks and she'd finally given in, if only to shut him up. He was cute. That's really all he had going for him.

Cute didn't trump homophobic, especially not after her favorite cousin Deion had just come out of the closet to his conservative Baptist parents last month. He'd stayed with her during the fallout. Saying gay men or gay sex was gross?

Strike three. And she was out of there.

Jada continued to mentally berate Ryan as she wandered around the concession stands. Ryan had driven so she had to call her friend Viv for a ride. But Viv was working so she'd have to wait an hour or more before she got there. Better waiting an hour or two than spending another minute in Ryan's company. She bought a bottle of water and started to wander around the stadium to kill time.

From the stands she heard shouting, applauding, cheering; for twenty minutes after that she watched happy fans pour from the stadium. Sounded like the home team won. Good for them. She was no baseball fan but the boys she saw out on the field were all young, fresh faced and sexy as hell in their tight white pants, ball caps and jerseys. She should have dated a baseball player in college. Maybe it wasn't too late. Only twenty-seven, she could still pass for twenty-two or twenty-three. More time passed, and she grew bored. Maybe she'd check out the locker room and see if any of the players were still around for her to meet. Wouldn't that be the best revenge on Ryan? Dating one of his home-team heroes...

Worth a shot.

It took a while but finally she found the Devils' locker room. The game was long over and it looked deserted. Minor league teams clearly didn't have the money for anything as fancy as security guards.

Inside the locker room, Jada nosed around. Nothing much to see. Just lockers, shoes, dirty uniforms and towels strewn everywhere. Wandering into the shower room, she smiled at all the hair product lying around. Straight or gay, all men wanted to look good. Jada froze when she heard voices—two of them, both male. Not wanting to get arrested for trespassing, she hid in one of the shower stalls.

Two men stepped into the shower area—one in uniform, the other in black track pants and a white T-shirt.

"Is it bad?" the man in track pants asked. "Where's it hurt?"

"Inner thigh. I think it's just a strain," said the younger player—number 29 himself, Flak Gordon.

"Let's make sure it's nothing worse."

They stepped into the room right across from the shower stalls. Through the other side of the curtain, Jada could peer in and see everything. It seemed to be some kind of therapy room. A padded leather table only about four feet high constituted the only furniture in the room. A plaque on the door read EVAN CHRISTOPHER, SPORTS THERAPIST.

Flak started to strip out of his uniform. Jada winced at the black bruise that covered the left side of his back where the fastball had struck him. Other than the bruise, however, Flak's body was flawless—broad shoulders, well muscled and sturdy, and yet not an ounce of fat on him. A young man's body. The trainer, Evan, was sexy in his own right, too. Slightly taller and about five years older, Evan wore wire-rimmed glasses on his handsome, intelligent face and had a seductive five o'clock shadow on his sculpted lower jaw.

Evan handed Flak a towel. The ballplayer, now completely naked, lay flat on his back on the table. He covered his groin with the towel, which made Jada almost groan with frustration. She couldn't see the action through a damn towel.

At the sink, Evan washed his hands and doused them with some kind of liquid. He slid his hands under the towel and started to massage Flak's left inner thigh.

"Did you slide?"

"Like a motherfucker," Flak said.

Evan grinned.

"Hope it was worth it."

"We won."

"Then it was worth it. How's this feel?" Evan asked as his hand slid deeper under the towel.

"Good," Flak said, slightly panting.

"Good?"

"I mean, it hurts." Flak seemed to realize "Good" was not the right answer. "I mean your hand...fuck."

Flak glanced down and Jada noticed that the towel over his groin had risen a few inches.

Evan didn't miss a beat.

"Happens all the time. Don't worry about it."

"I'm sorry."

"Don't be," Evan said, still massaging Flak's inner thigh. "The straightest guys on the planet get erections during massages and therapy. Especially on groin muscles. I won't take it personally."

"Thanks, Evan." Flak laid his head back down again. His chest heaved with a slow breath. He seemed to be willing his erection away. It wasn't working.

"Unless it is personal."

"What?"

Evan stared straight at Flak with a little smile on his lips.

"I've been counting, Flak. This is the fifth time you've come to me with injuries in the past two weeks. You step into heaters, slide when you don't need to slide…Are you *trying* to get on my table?"

Flak didn't answer at first.

"You know I'm gay, right?" Evan asked, his voice soft and soothing. "I don't care if you're into me or just into playing hard on the field, but if you're getting yourself hurt so I'll touch you, that's got to stop. Now are you really hurt or are you just trying to get my attention?"

"I don't know. Do I have your attention?" Flak asked. Jada ached with sympathy. She could hear the uncertainty in his voice.

"Does this answer your question?" Evan moved his hand under the towel and Flak's shoulders rose off the massage table.

"God, yes."

When Evan pulled off the towel, Jada saw he had Flak's erection in his hand. He stroked slowly with a full-handed grip as Flak rose up on his elbows and watched himself being touched.

"Is this okay?" Flak asked, still staring at Evan's hand on him. "You and me doing this?"

"No rules about players and trainers not getting involved. Of course, no one would ever dream a player would want to."

"I want to. God, do I want to…"

"You've done this before, right?" Evan asked, concentrating his attention on the tip now.

"Yeah. I dated someone in college. Just with the team, I'm not out yet."

"It's okay. You're out to me. That's a good start."

"Thanks. And thanks for that," Flak said, smiling at the sight of Evan still rubbing his erection.

"You want more than this?"

Flak nodded. "I've been leaning into pitches for two weeks trying to get to you, Evan. I want all of you I can get."

"Then you get all of me," Evan said as he brought his mouth down to Flak's. They kissed hard and deep, with Evan's hand clasped tightly around Flak's penis. Jada couldn't stop herself from lifting up her skirt and slipping a hand into her panties. She dipped her index finger into her vagina, covering it with her own wetness. She felt hollow inside, hollow and hungry and intensely aroused.

Evan kissed his way down Flak's chest and stomach as the ballplayer panted. The panting turned into a muted groan as Evan brought his mouth down onto him, taking every inch of Flak deep into his mouth.

As he sucked, Evan caressed Flak's long muscled legs and hips while Flak laid his hand lightly on the back of Evan's neck. Jada had never seen anything more erotic than these two men lost in desire for each other. They were both obviously strong men who could take care of themselves in a fight, but their mouths and hands on each other were gentle, almost tender. Jada could only watch and stroke her clitoris.

"Please..." Flak forced the word out as Evan moved his mouth up and down, licking every inch of him.

"Please what?" Evan grinned up at Flak.

"Do you top?"

Evan nodded, his hand stroking Flak. "You want me in you?"

"So fucking much," Flak breathed.

"Can't say no to that."

Evan stepped away from the table and rooted around in a black duffle bag on the floor. He pulled a condom and a tube of lubricant from the bag.

"You come prepared," Flak said, sounding relieved and impressed.

"I also come hard. And I come inside. And I come often."

"I love baseball, but seriously, this should be American's pastime." Flak laughed as he laid his head back on the table.

Evan pulled his glasses off and laid them on his duffle bag before stripping out of his shirt. Before his hands on Flak were gentle and careful. Now he grabbed the ballplayer's legs and shoved them to his chest.

"Stay there," Evan said with a wink. That wink nearly sent Jada over the edge. Her vagina spasmed with desire. She couldn't believe she was here watching these two beautiful men during their first time together. It was wrong to spy on them and she knew it. But revealing herself now would ruin the moment for them.

Flak wrapped his arms under his knees to hold his legs against his chest while Evan popped the lid on the lube. After putting a thick coating of the clear gel on his hand, Evan started to work two fingers into Flak.

"Good?" Evan asked as he moved his hand slowly in and out.

"God damn," Flak breathed.

"I guess that's good then. And this?"

Evan turned his hand and Flak flinched.

"Jesus, I almost came from that." Flak half-laughed, half-grunted the words.

"They give us a lot of anatomy training. Women have their G-spot. We have ours. Again?"

"Please."

Slower this time, Evan pushed his two fingers into Flak. From where Jada stood, it looked like he was moving his hand in and up. He made small tight circles as Flak closed his eyes and softly moaned from obvious pleasure. If she could, she would have moaned, too.

"That's amazing," Flak said, his eyes still closed.

"You feel amazing. I can't wait to get in you."

"You don't have to wait."

"You sure? How's that strained groin doing?"

"Never felt better."

Evan pulled his fingers out of Flak and shoved his track pants and underwear down to his knees. Quickly and expertly he ripped open the condom package and rolled it on in only seconds.

He positioned himself between Flak's thighs and slowly started to push in inch by inch.

Once inside, Evan settled against Flak, their naked chests touching. Their mouths met in a desperate kiss as Evan's hips pumped against Flak over and over again.

Jada stared, mesmerized by the sight of the two men together, their mouths and tongues and bodies intertwined. Evan's shoulder blades moved with each thrust, his back arching and bowing as he worked himself deeper and deeper inside Flak. For his part, Flak could do nothing in his current position but lie there and take it from Evan, who seemed to be in no hurry to reach the end of this encounter. His thrusts were slow and hard and Flak took a quick breath in each time Evan pulled out and penetrated him again.

While she watched, Jada worked her clitoris harder and faster, desperate for release. She envied Flak for the cock inside him. She'd kill to get fucked right now. As quietly as she could, she pushed her panties down her thighs and raised a foot to the shower wall. With her left hand, she pushed three fingers deep inside herself, pressing the knuckles into her own G-spot, while her right hand continued to tease her clitoris. It took all her concentration to stay silent as she filled herself up with her own fingers.

"I want to fuck you forever," Evan said before biting Flak's chest.

"Someone's gonna need this table eventually."

"We should move this party to my place then. Or yours."

"I don't care as long as you don't stop doing that."

"You mean this?" Evan slammed his hips into Flak and Flak gasped.

"That."

"Did that hurt?" Evan asked. "You winced."

Flak shook his head. "Your cock doesn't hurt. I just have a big damn bruise on my back."

"Shit. Forgot about the bruise."

Evan pulled out of Flak.

"You don't have to stop. Seriously," Flak said, rolling up on the table.

"I'm not. Just changing positions. Come here." Evan took Flak by the wrist and made him stand at the end of the table.

Evan kissed Flak once, long and lustfully, before turning Flak around.

"Bend over and hold onto the edge of the table," Evan ordered. Flak complied instantly. Jada watched Evan angle his erection and push it back into Flak. He made a few practice thrusts before wrapping his arms around Flak's chest and pounding into him. Flak clung to the table as Evan pushed and pushed against him, this time without his prior patience. It was all need now—need and hunger and two bodies joined together.

Evan wrapped a hand around Flak's erection again as his thrusts increased in speed and intensity.

"Come...please..." Flak begged. "I want you to come while you're in me. I've wanted that for weeks."

Evan was too far gone in ecstasy to respond. All he could do was thrust so hard into Flak even Jada winced. Low grunts, sounds almost like pain, escaped Evan's throat as he rammed into Flak. Jada couldn't wait anymore. As Evan came with a few final brutal thrusts, she came, too. Her vagina contracted around her hand, her clitoris pulsed against her fingers, her whole body shook and shuddered with the most intense orgasm she'd had in years.

For a few seconds, Evan rested his forehead against the back of Flak's neck. But then he pulled out and pushed Flak back onto the table. He pushed the ballplayer's thighs apart, shoved his fingers inside him and brought his mouth down once more onto Flak's erection.

Flak writhed under Evan's mouth, grasping at the edge of the table.

He came so hard his body jackknifed. Jada came again so hard, she nearly slid to the floor.

"Fuck..." Flak collapsed back on the table and laughed tiredly.

"I think that's what we just did." Evan wiped his mouth with the back of his hand before kissing Flak.

"Can we do it again?" Evan smiled as he pulled off the condom and wrapped it in a tissue.

"We can. We should. We will. Just not here. We're lucky no one walked in on us."

"Oh shit, I didn't even think about that. I guess there are janitors around."

"There are—and who knows who else. Get dressed. We'll go to my place and talk."

"Just talk?"

"Well…just for starters." Evan kissed Flak again and Jada smiled. God, what a cute couple.

Between talking and kissing, it took Evan and Flak about ten minutes to get cleaned up and clear out of the therapy room. Jada waited another ten minutes to make certain the coast was clear.

She pulled her panties up and washed her hands in the sink. Surely Viv would be arriving for her any minute. She checked her phone. No missed calls. Not here yet. Good.

In a daze she wandered the stadium, still in shock that she'd gotten to live out her deepest fantasy, seeing two beautiful gay men having incredible sex right in front of her. She'd be getting off on those images for months.

Viv finally arrived and took Jada home. As soon as she was alone, Jada got out her vibrator and relived the entire scene— Flak's adorable nervousness, his embarrassment at his own arousal, then the two men kissing, touching, the first tentative penetration with fingers, the thrusting…

Monday at work the image of Evan inside Flak still consumed her thoughts. She was so distracted by them she didn't even hear Ryan approach her desk.

"Jada?"

"What?" she asked, annoyed at having her delicious fantasizing interrupted.

"What the hell happened? You disappeared at the game."

"I did."

"Why?"

"Because you're an insensitive homophobe whose mother never taught him how to treat a lady right."

"I'd treat a lady right if I ever met one."

"And that's why I disappeared on Saturday. Because on top of being a homophobe who doesn't know how to treat a lady, you're an ass."

"Whatever. Last time I go out with a baseball-hating bitch."

He walked away. She flipped him off.

As soon as he was gone, she Googled a phone number and dialed it.

"Devils' box office," came the voice on the other line.

"Yes. I'd like to buy season tickets."

MADAM SECRETARY

Jaye Markham

I love my job. I have sex with the most powerful woman in the world.

The buzzer in my pocket alerted me, just before I heard the *ding* of the elevator and voices in the hall. Hers was weary as she said good night to her aide. The door next to mine opened and clicked closed. I turned off the television and adjusted the lights. Pouring a glass of fresh water, I scanned the hotel room. I threw my robe across a chair. All was ready.

Within a few minutes—enough time for her to put down her attaché case, take off her skirt jacket and kick off her shoes—there was a knock on the adjoining door. I pulled it open to see my Madam Secretary.

There were slight smudges of fatigue under her eyes. Wisps of hair had come loose from a clasp and curled around her face. I closed the door while she set down her phone. I prayed we would be undisturbed. She deserved a few hours away from the demands of others. She turned and pulled me into her arms, laid her head in the crook of my neck and sighed.

"I'm so glad to be here. Finally."

I drew in the now-faint smell of her citrusy perfume. I unpinned her soft hair and ran my fingers through it. I stroked her silky curls and her strong back, soothing her after a long day. It was nearly midnight and she had left our rooms at six-thirty that morning. Not unusual for when we were on the road. *On the road* is a misnomer, though; it's more like *flying through a country.* Yesterday and today had been Paris, and if the schedule didn't change, in two days we would be in Berlin. That's how it is when you have a secretary of state whose concerns literally span the globe.

"Would you like something to eat, Madam Secretary? The kitchen is open for another hour."

"No, thank you. I'm not hungry for food," she said, her breath tickling my neck.

"Then, what may I do for you tonight, Madam Secretary?

For a moment she didn't speak. When she stepped back, her eyes were dark with emotion, her face stern. "It depends. Did you draw my bath, or have you been lazing around the hotel all night?"

She held me by the shoulders with warm hands, as her gaze started at my feet and rose up my body. She took in my bare feet, my black thong, and the lacy black silk bra that barely contained my full breasts. My nipples jumped to attention as her gaze caressed me. I ached for her touch, but I knew it could be a long wait.

"No, Madam Secretary, I did neither," I said in a soft voice. "You buzzed earlier that you wanted something different." Although a hot, relaxing bubble bath, or a full-body massage, might have been her preference on other days, I'd learned from the evening news that her day had not gone as planned. Treaty negotiations had bogged down between the United States and a Middle Eastern country. Her buzz of number nine had told me she needed to work off her frustration rather than soak it away. She was not planning to use the hotel's stationary bike.

She grabbed me by the nape of my neck and pulled me closer. Her other hand seized my breast as her mouth took mine in a bruising kiss. I tasted raspberry, knowing she had probably popped a candy in her mouth while in the elevator. She rubbed her thumb back and forth over my nipple.

I whimpered.

While her tongue tangled with mine, she yanked my bra up, and pinched my nipples. She drew back and flashed me a wicked grin before leaning forward to bite the skin over my collarbone.

I would wear her mark tomorrow.

She rasped her tongue over a nipple, wetting it before drawing it into her mouth. She sucked and tugged. She rolled my other nipple between her fingers.

I moaned. My legs were weakening.

She pulled her head up to look me in the eyes. Her lips quirked. She glanced down and no doubt saw the pulse I knew was pounding in my neck. With a satisfied smile she said, "You're creaming in your panties now, aren't you?"

"Yes, Madam Secretary," I managed to say. I swallowed hard, not certain what was coming next.

Reaching around me, she unfastened my bra and tossed it aside. She ran her smooth hands down my arms. Hooking a finger in the band of my thong, she tugged me toward the bed. "On your knees," she said in the authoritative voice she normally uses in front of Senate committee inquiries.

46

I knelt on the cool, sweet-smelling sheets with my toes near the edge of the bed, my back straight and proud. She pushed my upper back down with one hand. I rested on my elbows. I turned my face to watch, but she was quicker. She slapped my left buttock. Hard.

I yelped and blinked back the moisture in my eyes.

"Who's in charge?"

"You are, Madam Secretary," I said, embarrassed by my quavering voice.

She grabbed the thong and tore it off my body. She stepped away and reached for the tube of lube on the nightstand, then smoothed her hand across my back. She spread my cheeks, ran lube around the tight opening and worked her finger inside.

I gasped.

"Now I have you right where I want you," she growled.

Uh-oh. The meeting must have been worse than I suspected.

She held me by my left hip while she plunged her finger in. Out. In. I trembled with excitement as moisture ran down my legs. The musky scent of my arousal filled the air.

I groaned.

"I love fucking you in your ass," she said with a husky voice. "I love how excited you get."

I groaned again.

She cleared her throat and withdrew her finger until only the very tip was inside. "I can't hear you. Tell me you want me to fuck your ass."

"Yes, yes. Please fuck my ass, Madam Secretary," I panted out.

She thrust her finger in, twisting and turning all the way.

I nearly came.

"You may not come until I say you can," she commanded. She always knows how close I am.

"Yes, Madam Secretary," I gasped. I bit my lip and tried to steady my breathing. No telling how long she would make me wait. Damn those diplomats.

She twisted and wiggled her finger as she slowly, quarter inch by quarter inch, withdrew. Her silky hair caressed my skin as she ran her tongue up my back—my erogenous zone. She brushed kisses over my shoulder, before trailing her tongue down my spine once again.

I whimpered; all my nerves were on fire.

She plunged in fast and hard, her knuckles hitting my flesh. *Oh my god. I'm going to die right here.*

She pulled out—gradually. Tormenting me. Teasing me. Tantalizing me.

"Please, Madam Secretary. I need to come." I wasn't too proud to beg. Not when she was so unmercifully screwing my ass. So wonderfully. So completely.

She gave a throaty laugh—then plunged in again. I shook with need.

"Please," I croaked.

She released my hip and ran soft fingers across my stomach to my moist folds. She swirled the moisture all over my clit. I bit my lip, tasting blood.

"You're so wet," she said in a husky voice that turned me on even more, if that was possible.

"You do that to me, Madam Secretary," I somehow managed to say.

With one finger buried deep in my ass, she sank two other fingers into my cunt.

"Yes! Yes," I sobbed in relief.

All fingers stilled.

I drew in a breath, remembering. "Yes, please, Madam Secretary. Please fuck my cunt."

"Excellent." She resumed. With a slow motion, she would withdraw the finger from my ass, while thrusting two into my cunt. Plunging one finger in while she withdrew the others. Back and forth. In and out her fingers moved with a slicking sound. The scent of my arousal blended with what I knew was her scent.

I tightened around all her fingers, knowing I was close.

"May I come please, Madam Secretary?" *Please, please don't make me wait any longer.*

"You may," she said as she pushed in and out of my two holes.

Waves of pleasure raced through my body as I came. I yelled her name. Spasms rocked me, and I came again. She trailed gentle kisses down my back and across my buttocks.

She withdrew all her fingers, grasped my hips and flipped me over. She pushed up her skirt, climbed onto the bed and straddled my thigh. Her wetness had seeped through her panties and coated my leg as she thrust against me. I wrapped my arms around her and pulled her closer. I kissed her until she moaned into my mouth, shook and collapsed on top of me. Her heart pounded against my chest as she drew in breaths. I pressed kisses against her moist forehead. I stroked her damp curls. After a few minutes, she rose up. No longer did her face appear haggard. Instead, her eyes twinkled and she smiled.

I love my job.

KITCHEN SLUT

Olivia Archer

I confess: my kink involves kitchenware. *Fucking* my kitchenware to be precise. Whisks, also called *whips* in the culinary world, are my favorite go-to devices. Their stainless-steel handles are perfect phalluses and the whipping ends come in a dazzling array of selections to tickle and tease. My whisk collection is proudly displayed on my kitchen wall because I find their shapes beautiful to view. And touch. And they make wonderfully convenient dildos. I don't want the vibrating, silicone rabbits sold at sex shops; useful utensils work best for me.

But it's impossible to fulfill my deepest needs alone. Heated honey dripped on my own nipples holds no thrill of anticipation, no surprise. Where is the lover who will bend me over the bar stool with my ass in the air and tightly tie my ankles and wrists to the chair with linen butcher's twine? I want to feel the smack of my favorite wooden kitchen paddle as it turns my cheesecake-hued cheeks the color of fresh strawberry granita. Alas, my last decent whisk man and I parted company last year, shortly before I moved here. I'm tired of sitting alone at the kitchen table, masturbating against the back of a beautifully curved soup spoon while checking my inbox. That's why I reluctantly joined one of those dating sites. You know, where you indicate the inane: dogs or cats, toilet paper up or down, favorite TV shows and movies. It's much too vanilla for my taste, but my kinky men couldn't get past their leather cuffs and collars and into my kitchen drawers.

The endless charades of this game annoy me. I mean, really. In truth, we are all just animals looking to mate. Except, as evolved animals, females don't just wait around with our rears in the air and moan for a male to mount us. No. We use other means to satisfy ourselves. My fetish just happens to involve objects found at your local high-end cooking store, and another set of hands adds a much-needed dimension to the equation. In my ad, I merely answered the turn-ons question with the words *whisks, spoons, and tongs.* Then I waited.

Men contacted me. Lots of men. They seemed to be looking at my picture, but I needed them to move past my short blonde hair and blue eyes, and be interested in my words because *they* were the true window to my soul. None of the men mentioned my kitchen kink in their responses. So, my reply to all was: "Hi. Thanks for contacting me. What do you think of my turn-ons?"

They disappeared into the ether. The ones that answered sent back responses along the lines of confused questions such as, "Do you mean like the kind you cook with?" Or, my favorite, "Is that the name of a band?" Uh, no. Well...not that I know of anyhow.

It was hopeless. These e-men just didn't speak my language. I deactivated my account to keep my sanity and get some of my spare time back. Online dating had been consuming my mornings and keeping me from one of my new Sunday morning activities: rolling out of bed early, all rumpled and warm, throwing on my worn jeans and a favorite shirt, then walking a mile to the little café near downtown.

After coffee and a pastry, it got even better. While the good people of the world were still at church, I walked farther into the shopping district and took a gander at the gadgets in the well-known kitchen store. You know the one. You throw their catalogues into the recycling bin after a quick glance. You've even bought something tasteful for your boss, who's a gourmet cook.

The same two employees had opened up shop each Sunday since I'd discovered this place. Connie, a cute salesgirl around my age, would yell, "Good morning, Laurel," as I entered, then follow me around. She was upbeat and always trying to draw me out. Though it took away from my shopping experience, I did look forward to listening to her chatter about everything under the sun. It was probably apparent that something was missing from my life, but I'm not sure she was picking up on what my desires entailed. She kept after me, playfully trying to get me to meet her and hang out at a bar, or go clubbing, but I'd done too much of both in my twenties and was over it.

Connie's boss was there every Sunday morning, too. When he caught my eye, he would smile, his steely eyes intense but friendly. She'd refer to him mock-seriously as "The Manager," then roll her eyes at me. From his starting-to-gray temples, I guessed he was about ten years older than me, and trying to keep it professional since he never responded to Connie's lively taunts. She tried again today to draw him in, but he ignored us, focusing on something on the computer screen instead. She pointed at him and whispered a little bit too loudly, "He needs to lighten up."

Just then, another customer entered the store and Connie was diverted, trying to score a sale. I was glad to finally look around by myself. Autumn had arrived and the displays were promoting their holiday fare. I looked longingly at the turkey lifters, hoping mine would be doing more than lifting my Thanksgiving turkey. But in reality, no one would be tying me to my baker's rack and raking the turkey lifter tines down my back. I sighed and pulled myself out of that daydream, waving good-bye to Connie as I left the store.

The following Saturday was Halloween weekend and the time change. In a funk, I had blown off all outings and stayed home, handing out candy, and calling it a night around ten. Though the clock moved back, my body was up at its normal time, and I made my Sunday excursion to the café, but only got as far as the front door.

My walk downtown usually took me to the kitchen store as they were first opening. Today, I would have to kill an hour at the café, or just head home. Standing there was getting me nowhere; the season's chill was really starting to set in. I needed to move. I decided to stick with my routine and took my walk knowing the store would be closed but I could see if its window displays had changed.

As I glanced into my favorite store, I noticed "The Manager" fussing around in the back, dressed in his usual button-up shirt and business casual slacks. He saw me, so I gave a short wave and continued to walk on by. To my surprise, the door opened when I was about to round the corner. When I turned, he called my name and gestured me inside. I walked over and said, "Oh, no, it's okay. It just takes me a few days to get used to the time change."

"Please, come inside where it's warm. There's something you'll be interested in."

Lured by curiosity, I took him up on his offer, and felt a secret thrill at being able to shop before store hours. Maybe I *had* spent too much money here, to get this kind of indulgence. He was right, it was warm inside—very warm. I was a little startled when I heard him lock the door behind us but I figured Connie would soon round the corner and come bouncing over with her latest news.

He walked past me and began working on a display, spreading a beautiful jacquard tablecloth over a table and setting out a small bowl of olive oil, presumably to dip some bread for tasting. I felt comfortable perusing the store alone, without having to worry about touching the items in front of someone's watchful eye. With pleasure, I allowed myself the time to caress the clean curve of the large black KitchenAid stand mixer, and to palm the perfect weight of a Henckels knife. The metal items still held the chill of the night.

As I paused to ponder the tiny ceramic turkeys that held sexy little pumpkin-colored tapers, he came up behind me— very close behind me—and said, "Laurel, I have something that will interest you."

Turning, I gasped, because he was holding the biggest ball whisk I had ever seen. The handle was a good twelve inches long, with a girth that any man would envy. All I could muster verbally was, "Wow!" but my body responded like a trained animal and all of my senses came to full attention, awaiting pleasure.

We appreciated its beauty as he strummed the tines with his

thumb and said, "See, it's as finely tuned as any instrument."

The Manager stated that he had ordered this professional series model with me in mind since I had purchased all of their more unusual and interesting whisks. The sensitive hairs along the nape of my neck shivered in anticipation of those cold spheres prickling me.

"Yes, I collect them," I answered, as if justification was needed.

This whisk definitely qualified as a keeper. It was beautiful—the outer circle consisting of eleven tines with shiny, silver ball-tipped ends, and one tine with a large silver ball in the center. Seen head-on, it looked like eleven silver planets orbiting a sun. Stunning for its design and impressive for its size. The home cook would need some strength because the sheer weight of it would test your muscles as you whipped the cream into what my mother called *schlag* to top your perfectly spiced gingerbread.

He handed the whisk to me and watched as I considered the weight of it in my hand, then he asked, "Think you can handle it?"

I nodded. Oh, I could handle this indeed. It would be a lovely addition to my collection in the kitchen. I would for sure see if I could handle it in the bedroom. As soon as I got home. Maybe after heating up my body and mind with a lovely cup of hint-of-mint cocoa and a bit of erotica. Those cute little spheres on the whisk would remind me of his steady gray eyes as I whisked up some ecstasy.

Bringing the implement between us, he turned the handle toward me. At this angle it looked like a huge silver erection with a dozen antennae on the other end, something out of a sci-fi porn movie. Oh, yes, I was taking this baby home. But did

I offer to pay him for it, or was it a special gift for being such a valued customer? I didn't think I could fit something of that size in my ass comfortably, and giggled at the image I would make trying to fuck myself with something this big. Okay, enough with the daydream.

As I reached for my wallet in the universal *I'm-going-to pay-for-it* gesture, he stilled my hand and took the whisk from me. Then he carefully pressed its smooth handle against my warm lips. When I purred softly with pleasure, he responded with a knowing laugh. Walking over to the display he'd been working on, he lifted the bowl of olive oil, then spread the tablecloth on the floor behind the register so it was out of sight to any passersby.

"Laurel, lie down. We have thirty minutes before the store opens. It's time you learned how to properly use those whisks that you keep buying."

I obeyed wordlessly, going behind the register, kicking off my shoes and stretching out for this man whose name I still didn't know.

"Off with your clothes, Laurel. Every last thing." It was not a question.

I stripped, wondering if Connie was part of this.

The Manager carefully placed a silver serving tray with various items on it down on the floor next to me, then knelt between my legs and traced the tines around my erect nipples. It was comfortably warm down on the floor, which amplified the whisk's cool dance on my receptive skin.

When his eyes assessed every inch of my naked body, I decided I was his alone for this brief interlude. This angle gave me a great view of his hard-on, which was nicely tenting the front of his trousers. My hand reached out to stroke his cock, but he shook his head and said, "That's not on the menu today. *You* are."

Drawing circles on my skin with the whisk, he rubbed his way down to my closely cropped pubic hair and used the ball-tipped tines to gently push between my labia. My mind could hardly focus on anything except the throbbing in my pussy.

Slowly, oh so slowly, he used those tiny spheres to massage me; my swollen sex pulsated in response. I couldn't tell if five minutes had gone by, or fifteen, as the center of my world became the area on my skin where his whisk gently prodded into my folds. I raised my hips, pushing myself against the tines with as much force as I could, prodding the balls into my wet lips.

He stopped. *What?* I looked at him questioningly. Consulting his watch, he held up his finger in the universal *wait* signal and said, "I have time for this."

Looking over the serving tray, he chose an elegant bone-handled cheese knife, and caressingly moved the blunt side of the blade up from my ankle to my thigh. At this point I felt I must be leaving a puddle on his nice new tablecloth, but was beyond caring. Very carefully he turned the knife on edge, applied pressure and raised lovely little welts as he traced a pattern on my inner thighs.

Next, he brought out a dark red jar of jam the very same flavor I had discovered last summer during my trip to Italy. In his other hand, a gorgeous wooden spreader. He admired the spreader, stroked its fine finish, then apparently decided against it. Instead he rolled up his sleeves and dipped his fingers in the dark, fragrant Maraca cherry jam, spreading a small sampling of it across my taut stomach. As he lapped up a bit of jam, he let his teeth graze the edges of my belly button, and I moaned with delight.

Before I could form much of a coherent thought, he was

lubing up the business end of the giant whisk with the fragrant olive oil. The weight of the handle nudged my engorged clit and I eagerly spread my legs, willing him to enter me. Instead, he took his time, tracing a path with the smooth handle up my body, and bringing it to rest on my mouth, letting me taste the greenness of the olive oil mixed with the sweet tang of the jam and the heady saltiness of my own juices. It was the most amazing explosion of the senses.

Like an animal in heat, I lifted my hips up, grinding them against empty air, willing penetration. He laughed and said very slowly, "You *are* a kitchen slut." With each carefully spoken word he inched the enormous phallic handle of the whisk inside me.

I must have been holding my breath because when he began to thrust the whisk, I released an enormous sigh and met him with each stroke.

It was a bit embarrassing how fast I came, but I had been waiting for this far too long. My pelvic muscles clenched the whisk and rode it through the waves of my orgasm.

Slowly he slid it out of my pussy. I opened my eyes, spent and dazed.

He passed me a clean kitchen towel, then disappeared some-where in the store.

I felt transported to another place in time and fought to get myself together so he could open the store. After wiping down, I pulled on my clothes and peeped over the counter; I saw him setting up his display again, his sleeves neatly down, humming some tune to himself.

As much as I'd enjoyed our tryst, I felt a bit awkward about how to end it. Did I walk over and thank him? Would I ever be able to set foot in here again?

He went into the back room. I considered darting out, but he quickly returned wearing a mischievous grin. In his hand, he had a bag from the store with the whisk inside, wrapped as neatly as any exquisite purchase would require.

"Here, Laurel, it's yours. Enjoy."

I took his cue and followed him to the door, exiting with my bag in hand and my pussy still pounding in aftershock.

When I got back to my place I went directly to my bedroom and ripped open the package. The enclosed note said, *By the way, my name is Ben. I have a delicious new salted-caramel chocolate sauce, and a gelato paddle that leaves lovely marks. Call me.*

I did.

Just Once

Jocelyn Dex

Mira stood outside the hotel room, taking slow, deep breaths, trying to quell the shaking in her hands and summon the courage to knock on the door.

At forty-eight, Mira was a widow. A widow who'd never fantasized during sex, feeling as though it was akin to cheating on her husband. At least, that's how he'd made her feel when she'd wanted to spice up their lackluster lovemaking by talking about their fantasies. He'd made her feel as if fantasizing was dirty, wrong, perverted and unfaithful. Being a good wife, she kept her fantasies in check and settled for whatever she got in the bedroom.

Once he'd passed and she'd grieved, Mira experienced the best orgasm of her life as she masturbated and allowed the three faceless men to ravish her body. In her mind, they licked her, fucked her, did all manner of things to her she'd never experienced, and she freaking loved it.

Since then, she couldn't put it out of her mind. Could she do that in real life? Her cunt flooded every time she thought about it. She wanted it, was obsessed with it and needed to experience it once. Just once.

She'd left messages, under an assumed name, on a few online message boards. Of course, she'd received hundreds of replies. Most were downright nasty, but one stood out—an intelligently written offer to meet in a public place of her choosing to chat and decide if she wanted to go through with it.

She'd met the men two days ago. Early thirties—at least ten years her junior—good shape, clean cut. She'd almost backed out of the meeting, anxiety making her sick, but downed two strong cocktails before walking to the coffee shop down the street to meet them. Within fifteen minutes, she decided these men were her one shot at bringing her fantasy to life.

Mira took one last deep breath, steadied her hand and knocked on the door.

Jace opened it almost immediately, his bright smile and wickedly dark eyes greeting her. "C'mon in," he said, opening the door wider for her.

She fidgeted with the hem of her shirt as she stepped inside. Rand sat on the edge of the king-size bed in shorts and a tank top. He'd been in business clothes at their first meeting, so she hadn't been treated to a clear view of his muscular physique. His arms were so ripped, she wondered how many hours per week he spent in the gym.

Adam sat at the desk, clad in a white button-down that was open to the waist, and a pair of black jeans. His deep-blue eyes seemed to penetrate her. Her cheeks flushed, and her knees weakened when Jace clicked the door lock into place.

Rand jumped up, putting an arm around her waist. "You okay?" he asked.

Her skin heated at his touch and she nodded. His lips grazed her ear, sending shivers down her spine as he whispered seductively, "Are you ready, Mira?"

Not able to make her vocal cords work, she simply nodded again. Wasting no time, he kissed her, his tongue delving into her mouth. He pulled her against his body, the evidence of his arousal pressing into her stomach. Her pussy got wet at once.

Another body pressed into her from behind. It must have been Adam because as she glanced around Rand's shoulder, she saw Jace removing his clothes, his dark eyes on her. A gasp escaped her when Adam's hand slipped beneath her skirt, his fingers stroking her pussy through her drenched panties. Desire and need stabbed through her. This was it. She was actually here and going through with it. He snaked his fingers inside the flimsy fabric and ripped them off. Her legs quivered at the savage but sexy act.

Jace, completely naked, long thick cock standing hard and proud, tapped Rand on the shoulder. Instantly, Rand relinquished his spot and Jace filled in, kissing her throat, while Adam slid his finger through her wet slit. Jace raised her arms above her head and pulled her shirt off. He pushed the red-lace bra fabric to the side, exposing a taut nipple, sucking it into his mouth. Goose bumps danced on her skin. Rand, now naked, joined in and drew her other nipple into his mouth.

She moaned, disappointed, when Adam's heat disappeared, but it was only a few seconds before his nakedness molded to her back. She squealed when he slid down to his knees and licked the crack of her ass while shoving two fingers deep inside her. Jace slid down her body and lightly traced her cunt lips with his warm tongue.

Holy hell. Three men touching her, teasing her, overwhelmed her senses. She was going to explode. Her pussy cried out for

Jocelyn Dex

release as she shoved her hips forward. Jace took the hint and drew her throbbing clit into his mouth and sucked with a delicious pressure. She grabbed on to Rand for support as pleasure speared through her veins and muscles, lit her organs on fire.

Jace's tongue lashing her clit while Adam finger-fucked her drove her insane, her knees threatening to buckle, her body about to burst and unleash a downpour onto Jace's face. One more lick and she came undone, crying out and sagging into Rand's strong embrace.

Rand carried her to the bed and laid her down, curling up beside her, stroking her face. "Was that good for you, Mira?" he asked, his voice low and husky.

His hot breath on her ear made her shiver. Again she nodded, breath raging, heart pounding. God, she loved the skilled attention of these men.

"More?" he asked, his lust-filled amber eyes sparkling.

Her eyes squeezed shut as she breathed her first word since entering the room. "Please."

Rand held her torso as Jace and Adam held her legs. They gently flipped her over and guided her body so her chest lay on the bed and her legs hung down, feet touching the floor, ass in the air.

Jace massaged her slit with the head of his cock. The sensation made her groan and push up on her hands. Rand took advantage of her position and scooted forward on the bed, putting his cock in front of her face. "Suck me," he commanded.

She bent forward and complied, wrapping her lips around his cock.

She screamed around his dick as Jace slammed into her, his cock filling and stretching her. Over and over he rammed it home as she sucked Rand with vigor, the salty, tangy taste of his flesh delighting her senses, making her mouth water.

She growled at the sudden emptiness when Jace abruptly pulled out of her. He scooted onto the bed next to Rand, his cock, shiny with her juices, demanding attention. She took his cock into her mouth, tasting her arousal on him, as she stroked Rand with her hand.

Suddenly, her wanton cunt was filled again. Adam. Fucking her hard and fast. Goddamn, she'd never felt so hot, desirable, fulfilled.

"Easy," Jace said. "I'm about to blow."

Hearing that made her suck harder, faster. She wanted it. Wanted his come in her mouth. Wanted to please them as much as they pleased her.

"Okay," he groaned. "You asked for it." His body tensed, his cock turning to steel as he grabbed her hair, thrust his hips and unleashed a torrent of come into the back of her throat. She gagged but swallowed every drop, the salty, thick liquid marking her, making her his bitch.

She whimpered when Adam pulled from her cunt, the sudden emptiness staggering, but he pulled her to a standing position so Rand could rearrange himself. Adam guided her into a reverse cowgirl on Rand's cock while he positioned himself in front of her and guided her mouth to his dick while she gyrated on Rand.

In this moment, she was theirs to do with as they pleased because it pleased her. She needed to be taken, to live her fantasy. Their touches inflamed her, every nerve in her body screaming for more, more, more.

Rand's fingers dug into her hips, guiding her while she sucked Adam. She opened her eyes, wondering where her third fantasy man was, and found him watching, stroking himself, almost ready to join the fun for more. He winked at her and strode toward the action. She lost sight of him but felt his weight on the bed behind her.

She shrieked around Adam's cock as Jace's hot, wet tongue entered her asshole. She tensed and tightened around the sensual intrusion, her cunt clenching with need.

"Relax," Jace coaxed. "We're gonna give you everything you need." She felt him shift, and then he was coating her ass with a slippery liquid that made her hole tingle. She'd stopped being able to move her hips but Rand continued pumping into her. Overwhelmed by sensation, she almost lost her ability to suck Adam, but he kept his hands on either side of her face, encouraging her, silently commanding her to continue.

Her pussy instantly contracted and exploded when Jace worked a finger into her ass. "That's it," he coaxed, as her body spasmed, came apart. She never knew that could feel so good.

"Ah, fuck," Rand said. "I'm not gonna make it."

"Don't move," Jace ordered her. She did her best to comply.

After a few torturous moments, Rand let out a harsh breath. "Okay. Do it," he said.

Jace rubbed the head of his cock through her asscrack, until settling at her tight entrance. She tried to pull away from Adam's cock but he held her firm and gazed into her eyes, shaking his head. "You needed this, remember? Let go. Relax. We'll take care of you."

She whimpered when the head of Jace's cock popped past the outer ring. He stilled, allowing her to adjust. Her ass clenched around his cock as he reached around and found her engorged clit with his fingers. He squeezed and stroked it and began slowly moving his cock deeper into her ass.

The fullness was incredible. A cock in her mouth, one in her cunt and another in her ass. Goddamn. She was going to die from pure fucking ecstasy. She was aware of every inch of her body, everything alert, tingling, crying out for pleasure. She'd never felt so alive.

She renewed her sucking with vigor as Jace sped up his thrusts and Rand pumped into her cunt. She felt as if she was being split apart, and loved every sensation.

"Come for us, Mira," Adam grunted. "And we'll give you all we've got."

Jace increased the pressure and speed of his fingers on her clit.

Oh yeah. Her body shuddered, muscles knotting, tensing, a white-hot fire spreading out from her pussy and traveling through every nerve ending. The climax sent her reeling, her vision went dark and when she thought she couldn't take any more, she heard Adam's strained voice, "Now. Yes?"

Jace and Adam grunted agreement.

Adam exploded in her mouth, his come coating her tongue and throat. Jace shot into her ass and Rand tensed as his cock poured hot semen into her pussy. Her pussy, ass and clit spasmed in unison as they filled her, fucked her, fed her as her blood burned and her skin melted. Her breathing raged, heart pounded, trying to recover from the sexual onslaught.

Jace rolled over to the side, pulling her with him, his cock slipping from her ass, Rand's slipping from her pussy and Jace's slipping out of her mouth with a popping sound.

Her back was pressed against Jace's body as he ran his fingers down her side, leaving goose bumps in their wake. Rand rolled to his side, facing her, and massaged her calves. Jace lay down and brushed her sweat-slicked hair from her face. The sensual smell of their sex permeated the air.

She couldn't believe what she'd just experienced, her body limp and content from the intensity, ecstasy and exertion. They were all so attentive, knowing exactly what she craved, what she needed. How would she ever go back to "normal" sex?

Jace kissed her neck, then whispered in her ear. "You're perfect for us, Mira. Any time you need us, we're here for you."

She smiled, more sated than she'd ever been. She realized just once would never be enough.

Boat Rocking

D. L. King

I was on top, sitting on David's stiff cock, slowly rocking back and forth, riding him like you'd ride a horse at a slow walk. His hands were on my breasts, squeezing and kneading and playing gently with my nipples. My back was arched, eyes closed, head thrown back with my long, straight brown hair just brushing against the swell of my ass. As I was reveling in the sensations, I suddenly got this image of my hair bound tightly around David's cock and balls. Every move of my head would jerk his package. The little sounds he made—little moans and whimpers—drove me crazy. In my mind's eye, my hair had grown really long, Rapunzel long, and I used it as a leash to lead him around the room by his tight balls and erect cock. I pulled on the hair leash and saw the devotion in his eyes. I saw him mouth the word *please*, and my fantasy swept me into a sudden paroxysm of release.

Poor David. I collapsed on top of him, seriously done for the day, or at least the moment. I knew he hadn't come yet, but I couldn't help it. "Sorry, babe," I said.

"Wow. No, that's all right; I was watching you. You seemed, well, you were definitely somewhere else. What were you thinking about?"

I looked at him with half-lidded eyes, remembering his submissive expression—and then I really saw him, his sincere, questioning expression and thought, *No, I can't tell him that.* "Nothing," I said.

"I know you were fantasizing about something. C'mon, you can tell me. Were you thinking about Channing Tatum or something? It's okay, my fragile male ego can take it."

I looked at him again. Our sex life had never been down that road: dominant/submissive games, rough sex, sadomasochism. No, we were decidedly less adventurous. Everything was good the way it was. Why rock the boat? I shook my head, trying to clear the images that had burned themselves into my consciousness. "No, nothing really, just you." And it was true, really; I *was* thinking about him.

I put the whole thing out of my mind and got out of bed. I didn't think about my fantasy of dominating my husband again until a few days later, on the way to the grocery store. Sitting at a red light, I suddenly saw an image of him whimpering, his cock and balls bound tightly in black leather straps, and my hand pulling on those straps. My body shuddered and I almost came right there, in the car. It wasn't until someone honked that I realized the light had changed.

Things like that started happening. I'd be sitting at my desk, at work, and get an image of him on his knees, licking my pussy as I stood over him—and I could feel his tongue in me. Or I'd be cooking dinner and I'd get an image of a black leather whip or pair of handcuffs and I'd start thinking of how I'd use them on David.

One evening, I was in fantasyland while cutting vegetables for a stir-fry when David wandered into the kitchen. Coming up behind me, he put an arm around my middle and nuzzled my neck before slipping a hand under my dress. He stroked me, first over my underwear and then under it. "Babe, you're soaked. Those must be some pretty sexy mushrooms."

As his finger explored inside me, I shivered and leaned back against him, vegetables forgotten. When he brushed against my clit, I came.

"Jesus, Audrey, what were you thinking about?" he said.

"I don't know. Nothing." I turned to kiss him. "Go set the table, we're going to be eating in fifteen minutes." I pushed him away and thankfully, he went. *Like a good boy*, I thought. And then I wondered where the hell that had come from. Oh, but I knew where it had come from.

After dinner, sitting on the couch watching TV, I just couldn't keep it to myself anymore. My timing couldn't have been better. We were watching a *CSI* rerun, one of the ones with the dominatrix character. With my eyes on the television, I said, "Ever thought about BDSM?"

"What?"

I got a little braver. "Kinky sex. Ever thought about it?"

"Thought about it how? You mean doing it?"

"Yeah." I moved away from him, just a little.

"Not really, why? Do you want to…oh. Does this relate to the other day in bed? Is that what you were thinking about? Did you want to try some stuff? Hey, were you thinking about that in the kitchen earlier?"

I started to question the wisdom of bringing it up. "Well, I mean, maybe," I offered, noncommittally.

"Well, I never really thought about it," David said, "but

sure, we could try it. Like bondage or something?"

"Yeah," I said. My pussy got a little squishy. "We could try that."

And so that night, David brought a few ties he didn't wear anymore to bed with us.

Of course, he got it wrong. After we got undressed, he proceeded to tie my wrists together and then tie them to a middle slat of our headboard. I didn't say anything, thinking maybe this would turn out to be as good as my fantasies of dominating him.

He spread my legs and tied my ankles to slats in the footboard. "Is that okay?" he asked. "It's not too tight, or anything?"

"No, it's fine," I said.

He didn't seem to have any idea what to do with me after tying me up. He stroked my body and played with my pussy, which was barely damp. Then he decided that the best use he could make of me would be a forced blow job. Climbing up to my head, he began to guide his cock to my mouth. "Is this okay?" he asked, none too sure of himself.

"Um, sure," I said.

He fucked my mouth for a bit but didn't get fully hard. I thought it was unusual because he really likes oral sex. I have to say, it did absolutely nothing for me. I'd hoped that, if that was what he wanted, I'd be able to translate my fantasy to fit his, but it seemed this wasn't his fantasy either.

He reached down to my sex and found me mostly dry. "Honey, I don't think this is working. What am I doing wrong? Can I untie you?"

He untied my ankles and then my wrists and we lay next to each other, staring at the ceiling. "Sorry, Aud, I guess I wasn't doing it right. Neither of us seemed to get much out of it. Hell, you were wetter slicing mushrooms than having my cock in your mouth."

"It's okay," I said.

"No, I want to make you happy. Can you just tell me about your fantasy?"

"You *do* make me happy, sweetie."

"I know," he said, "but just tell me what you want."

I silently counted to ten and then thought about it. I didn't want to screw up what we had. But he obviously wanted to please me. After all, he'd tried what he thought I wanted without any discussion. I should just be brave about it.

"So, what you did," I began, "that wasn't what I was thinking about."

We were on our backs, lying next to each other. He turned on his side and said, "What were you thinking about?"

"Well, I was thinking about doing it to you."

"What do you mean?"

I figured I'd come this far; it was make or break now. We'd probably be fine, and if he wasn't into it, I'd just never bring it up again. I started to tell him about my original fantasy: I told him about the whole hair thing: about binding his cock and balls in my hair and leading him around by a hair leash. I noticed his breathing had become a little erratic. I looked down at his cock, which had grown long and hard. I reached for it—wrapped my hand around it—and continued to tell him the rest of my fantasies about the handcuffs and binding his cock and balls in tight leather straps. I stroked him as I talked about black leather whips I'd seen online and how I'd thought about making him submit to me and service my pussy on his knees.

His cock had been dribbling precome freely for a while. I'd used it to lubricate the hand job I was giving him. The more I talked about my fantasies, the harder he got. The harder he got, the wetter I became. His eyes were open wide as he seemed to hang on every word. He didn't interrupt, but he breathed more and more deeply.

Completely soaked, I couldn't stand it anymore. I pushed him onto his back and climbed on top, guiding him into me. Once positioned, I sat down hard, impaling myself on his cock. I could feel him pulsing inside me.

"Oh, god, Audrey," he said, "I don't think I can hold out." I didn't think I could hold out either, at that point, so I started to fuck him slowly, but soon sped up. Panting like a sprinter, I came quickly, squeezing him in the vise grip of my cunt. He followed right after. "That was so fucking hot. I had no idea," he said, cuddled up beside me.

David stood by the bed, wearing nothing but his new collar. It was a shiny, heavy-link, stainless-steel chain with an ingenious locking system. It looked like a regular necklace, but could only be opened by a special key I kept in my bedside table. It hadn't come off since I'd put it on a month ago, on his birthday.

I used a tiny Allen wrench to open and then fasten a heavy stainless-steel ball stretcher, with metal rings on either side, above his testicles. It didn't take any time to coax him to erection, after which I buckled a leather harness tightly around his cock. "Hands and knees, on the bed now, David," I said. I was getting wetter and wetter. "Lean on your forearms and push your butt up for me. That's right. Spread your legs a bit more." I ran my hand over his bottom and reached under him to fondle his tightly bound balls. He groaned, but didn't say anything. I clipped weights onto the rings on his ball stretcher, pulling his sac down, away from his body. Shiny red skin stretched tightly over his imprisoned balls. I teased them lightly with my fingertips and he very audibly sucked in a breath. "Mmm," I responded.

I stepped into my new harness with its flesh-colored cock jutting from my pelvis. Though anatomically correct, it was a bit smaller than David's cock. After all, we'd just started opening up his ass for fucking. It would be a while before I would deem him ready for a cock the size of his own member. After all, I wasn't a sadist—well, not really.

I climbed onto the bed, behind him, and lubed him up before sensuously running my fingers back and forth over his open anus. With each pass over his open hole, he moaned, and with each moan, more and more moisture dripped from my pussy. I gently pushed a finger inside him and felt him contract around it. "That's right, David, breathe," I said, as I slowly fucked him with first one finger, then, when he was ready, with a second. I added more and more lube until it began to drip from his open hole, onto his stretched balls.

Up to this point, I'd only used smaller, smooth dildos in my harness. This time would be his first "real" fuck. I pulled my fingers from him. "Ready for me, baby?" I asked.

He nodded. "Yes, Ma'am."

I brought the tip of my cock up to his opening and rubbed it in the lube before slowly pushing it inside. I pushed in just past the head and stopped until his breathing slowed before pushing in a little farther. It took a little while, but finally I was balls deep inside my panting husband. "How's that, honey?"

"Fuck me, please," he said, between gritted teeth.

Hands on the sides of his hips, I slowly withdrew and then even more slowly pushed back in to the music of his moans. Once he became acclimated, I slowly began to speed up my thrusts until he actively pushed back against me, spurring me to fuck him harder. The harder I fucked him, the more the weights on his ball stretcher bounced, causing his balls to swing forward and back with each thrust of my body. The sight made me gush.

Ass in the air, his entire chest was now on the bed, arms over his head, hands gripping the slats in the headboard to keep his body from sliding forward as I fucked him harder and harder. "Oh, my god," I said, "that's it; I can't wait any longer." And I pulled out of him completely.

"No. Oh, no. Please, please don't stop," he moaned. "Oh god, please don't stop."

"On your back, legs spread," I ordered. "Now!" He whimpered but got into position while I quickly shed my harness. "Can you smell how hot you made me?" I turned my back to him and straddled him, pushing my pussy into his nose and mouth, painting him with my arousal. "Clean that up. Clean that up and make me come." I groaned as his tongue began to lap at my folds and quaked when it entered me. He clutched at my hips, driving his face deeper and deeper into me. He licked and sucked, growled and bit, as I actively fucked his face. It didn't take much to make me come at that point, but he didn't stop. He buried his tongue in me and ravaged me like an animal, his fingers digging into the flesh of my hips as I came again and then a third time. I knew I'd have finger-shaped bruises.

Once I'd collapsed on him, I unbuckled the harness encasing his penis and watched it spring up. With one hand on his straining balls, I wrapped the other at the base of him and licked and sucked the head of his cock. Once I had sufficient saliva, I went down on him as far as I could, teasing his balls while forming a tight suction on his cock, worrying the head with my tongue.

With my cunt still stopping his mouth, I felt his cock twitch and jump. I withdrew my mouth and pumped him hard with my hand. "Come for me, David. Come now," I said. A couple more pumps and he bellowed like a beast and shot into the air again and again until his cock finally lay limp against his leg. I opened the ball stretcher and told him he could remove it as soon as he was able and then I collapsed next to him, in bed.

"I love you," he whispered, his voice hoarse.

Our sex life is amazing and it all started with that crazy hair fantasy. Of course, I couldn't ever enact that fantasy. Not being Rapunzel, if I'd wrapped him in my hair, I would have ended up tethered too close to him to do anything. But now, when he's bound and helpless, I do tease him with my hair. And he invariably makes those sounds—the ones I heard in my fantasy. And those little whimpers and moans are music to my ears.

THE SLEEPER'S BEAUTY

Jade A. Waters

C arrie had never understood anal.

She wished it weren't so, and that she, like her girlfriends, could share the fascination with it that they all seemed to have. Inevitably, one of them would end up talking about it whenever they got together—how someone's man bent her over and took her in the ass so expertly she wailed and cried and blah blah blah—but for the life of her, Carrie couldn't fathom what the big hubbub was all about.

Even with Andrew wanting it over the years, she couldn't quite muster up the enthusiasm. He'd been so patient the few times they'd tried it, talking her through with the kindest, most encouraging words of love. And oh, what a good sport she'd been—her hands curled into tiny fists as he slicked the oil over her cheeks and down her crack, then massaged her until she was completely aroused and he could ease himself into her tight bud. She'd buried her face into the comforter as he thumbed her clit and gently took her ass, but as she contended with the pleasure of his fingers against the annoyance of his roaming cock, she knew he could still hear her whimpering and fussing. After, neither of them had been screaming for an encore.

Despite all of this, the idea kept sneaking into Carrie's mind. She'd find herself watching old reruns of "Friends" while Andrew tapped away on his laptop beside her, her breath held as she pondered what it would feel like for him to really thrust into her backside with that firm, sexy cock of his. She suspected it was a matter of getting the circumstances right—it had taken her thirty years to love Brussels sprouts, after all, so maybe the delights of anal were a refined taste she had yet to develop.

She'd been reading all sorts of magazines and books on the act, too, bookmarking pages and leaving the literature open on the table, much to Andrew's amusement. She'd even taken to asking her girlfriends for tips on the best lubricants, environments and techniques to make it work.

When Carrie announced her budding interest at dinner two weeks ago, Andrew had chewed the bite of pork chop in his mouth until it was practically liquefied. He'd stared at her for a long minute after he swallowed, then shook his head.

"Sweetheart, I love you the way you are. Stop worrying about this. You're getting all obsessive again, and you don't need to."

He'd gone back to his book and Carrie—not quite ready to launch the adventure just yet—had continued to eat in frustrated silence.

Then last weekend, when she and Andrew fell into bed drunk and frisky after their neighbors' party, she begged him to try again. They fumbled around in the dark for a bit, Andrew nestling the head of his cock right up against her before she started urging him on in hungry shouts of "Do it!

I'm ready, baby, go! Stick it in!" They were the same kinds of demands she'd made when they'd first had sex in their early twenties—only this time her calls were over anal, and Andrew laughed and rolled away from her.

"You hate it, Carrie. I'm not going to make you," he said. Then he'd passed out.

So tonight, Carrie decided, things were going to be different. She was determined to make it happen. She couldn't take one more "Friends" episode thinking about the hard slide of his dick all the way up inside her until she cried like the girls said she would, and she'd be damned if fear of a little ass play was going to keep her from knowing all the pleasures she could have.

Knowing Andrew would catch on to her eager glances and deter her yet again, Carrie made him his favorite meal—a pot roast slow-cooked in his preferred beer with a side of mashed potatoes, and two glasses of wine. He'd devoured the dish with that twinkle in his eye that managed to say *You're wonderful* and *I love you* all at once. After dinner, she walked him to the bed and stripped off her clothes, running her hands all over herself in the most provocative ways she could think of until he chuckled and pulled her down on top of him.

"What is with you, lately?" he said. He wrapped his hands around to cup her ass, then tugged her against the bulge in his boxer-briefs. "I mean, seriously. You're talking anal and attempting stripteases. Settle down, Carrie."

She sighed, helping his motion with a long grind that made him groan. "I'm trying something new here. I'm adding spice! Is it really that bad?"

"God, no. But you don't have to do these things you don't want to do." Andrew took her hands between his and lifted them to his lips so he could kiss her fingertips. Then he shifted his hips up and rubbed against her. "I love having sex with you as is. And I'm tired, hon. Let's just do it normal."

Carrie snatched back her hands. "I want to try something new! What kind of man complains about getting what he's been asking for? Suck it up and enjoy it already!"

With that she scooted low on his legs, running her kisses like she usually did all over his belly and chest. Andrew clicked his tongue, the belittling sound urging her on, and Carrie grumbled before yanking off his underwear. She admired his cock at full alert, then wrapped her mouth around his crown.

"Oh, babe," he uttered. "That's perfect. Just perfect."

Carrie worked his shaft, running her tongue along the base as she knew he liked, then teasing his balls with both of her hands. This was only a precursor in her mind, because she'd already grown wet at the thought of what was to come.

And dammit, she was ready.

Carrie licked and sucked her husband, running her mouth along his length while sneaking one hand back to touch herself. He was too preoccupied to notice, and when she slid her finger inside her slick opening, images of him filling her special, secret hole crept through her head. She moaned against him and dragged her hand over her clit in small circles that stoked the heat way up inside her.

Andrew, meanwhile, grew quiet. Carrie swallowed him fully, making sure to bang him against the back of her throat in the way that always made him squirm, but he didn't respond. When she looked up, his eyes were closed and his lips were parted as though he was about to snore. She pulled away.

"Andrew! Has it really come to this?"

He jerked awake and reached for her. "No, no, it's fine. I'm just a little sleepy. You made pot roast, honey. It's heavy."

She growled, the excitement raging inside her as sleepiness threatened to damper her plans.

"Do you want me to stop?"

"Hell, no," he mumbled. "Climb on me, I love it. Fuck me to sleep."

Carrie flicked her clit once, then again, leaning back far enough to take in the view of her husband half-asleep with his dick straight up in the air. Then she glanced over at the night-stand where she'd left a giant bottle of lube.

Quickly, she snatched up the bottle. She poured the liquid into her hand and rubbed it over Andrew's penis, while he curled his fingers around her hip.

"Get on me, Carrie. I can't wait."

She poured more lube onto her other hand and clapped it against her sex. Her tension was already peaking as she fingered herself a few times. She dragged the wetness down her slit and to the back, probing the tight muscles with her fingertips. Something about the way Andrew's shaft stood high as could be while his eyes were half-closed made her quiver, and she used that to fuel herself as she eased one finger inside her bud. With all the lube she had on her fingertip, it was easy to moisten the entrance. Carrie took a deep breath, pushing her finger higher while she gripped Andrew's throbbing rod, and when he started nodding and moaning, she ran her finger in and out, in and out, the rhythm making her tremble.

"Now, baby," Andrew said. His words were sharp yet subdued mumbles that warned her she didn't have much time before he fell asleep, so she climbed over him. She debated making it easy and sinking him into her pussy instead, but as she shoved her second knuckle past the rim of her back hole, the idea of finally getting this ass thing down really gnawed at her.

Carrie positioned herself so Andrew's crown rested against her tender opening. She glided her hand over him in a firm, squeezing tug, then whispered, "Do you mind, sweetheart?"

"Never, honey. I'm yours."

Carrie guided his penis past her barrier. The pressure was intense, far greater than her finger a moment before, but she eased until his tip anchored inside her. She moaned, taking a few sharp inhalations while Andrew nodded with half-slitted eyes.

"Yeah. Damn, you feel good. So tight," he muttered.

Carrie grinned, pleased she'd made it this far and noting the pulsing she felt along her sensitive ridges. With him so sedate she could control exactly how far she took him in. The power made her feel beautiful. She clenched her vaginal muscles. They buzzed with the promise of a full-mind orgasm takeover, which spurred her on. Before she knew it, she'd taken half his length inside her. Andrew groaned as she put her lubed-up hands to use, coating their intersection and taking him farther in. The fullness was daunting, but Carrie had grown so wet at the thought of knowing this joy once and for all that she now dripped all over his crotch.

"Andrew, this is kind of amazing," she whispered. He gave another low grunt and placed his hands back on her hips. Carrie closed her eyes to slip her fingers over her clit. It raged and swelled as she rubbed it, and she cried before dropping down, Andrew's cock kissing the highest reaches of her ass. The sensation brought the most surprising warmth into her pussy. "Oh wow…"

"Yeah," Andrew said. His sleepiness had taken over, and now he barely moved save for an occasional lazy squeeze of her hips. Carrie felt a shudder of guilt as she used her knees to lift herself up and down, but his moans kept right on coming, quiet yet present. She spread more lube along him and around her opening, her inhalations growing more spastic. Andrew jerked inside her and she heaved over him, riding and grinding ever faster against her fingertips.

She was losing herself in it—the building force, the warmth, the overwhelming urge that coiled and burned inside her. She felt like a goddess, panting and throwing back her head, so pleased she'd not only managed to take him in but that she was finally understanding it as she thrust and felt him at her own pace. She sank lower and rubbed her clit, then raised herself and stroked harder. His length tickled her depths and as the lube squished between them she started running her fingers everywhere—inside her cunt, along him, over her breasts, then back down to tease her own nub. Andrew made a slight gasp and Carrie growled at the way he swelled inside her ass. Suddenly, her orgasm struck, pummeling her senses and driving her to slam against him. "Yes!" she moaned. She pounded so hard she couldn't believe he was *in her ass* and she *liked it,* and when she forced herself all the way down, she howled, "Oh my god, Andrew, yes!"

She sucked in a breath and toppled over him, her body weak and her fingers numb. She kissed his belly while she caught her breath, then lifted her head to share her sated grin with her husband. Who had fully fallen asleep.

"Andrew?"

Immediately, the blood in Carrie's body rushed into her cheeks. She sat upright, her hands prunish, her pussy sopping—and his cock still solid and filling her ass.

"You're kidding," she muttered. Slowly, calmly, she eased herself off him and staggered into the bathroom for a warm, wet cloth. When she came back into the room, Andrew rolled onto his side. She wrapped the cloth around his shaft and he jumped. When he peeled open his eyes, she pinched her lips in embarrassment.

"What are you doing?"

Carrie dabbed at his skin. "I...um..."

Andrew shook himself. "Did I doze off?"

Her cheeks were so warm she could barely face him.

"Did you...?"

She nodded.

"Well, well, well," he said, chuckling. "I guess you like anal now, after all, huh?"

She tossed the washcloth at him. "I can't believe you fell asleep!"

Andrew grabbed her hand and tugged her back to the bed. He wrapped his body around her, letting his erection graze her from behind.

"I was awake. Awake enough for you to take me—but it's really no fair, you know. I didn't get to fully experience it."

"I didn't realize, and I was in the moment...and I—"

"Do you want to do it again?" He reached his hand over her hip, planting it squarely over her mound and pushing himself against her backside until she moaned. "I promise I'll stay awake this time."

Carrie giggled at her husband. He skimmed his fingers over the sensitive knot of her clit, then ran his lips over her neck in a series of hungry kisses that made fresh goose bumps break over her skin. She didn't know how much more she could take, but it did seem only fair.

"Yes," she whispered, gasping when he nudged himself between her cheeks.

Then Andrew reached for the lube.

Upstairs at the Ava

DelovelyOlive

It was early May, but already summer had draped itself over the pristine Arizona suburb I called home. It shimmered like a mirage on the highway blacktop as we drove across town to Poncho's, a local Mexican restaurant with the best sangria this side of the border.

"Remind me why we live here again?" Steve complained, cranking the AC up another notch.

I ignored my husband's question and just enjoyed the full blast of icy air blowing through my bangs. The scenic desert rushed beside us as we sped along toward our destination. I gazed out my window at the endless blue above me and the seam of earth below, cracked and baking under the relentless sun; all the while thoughts of her walked in silent footsteps across my mind.

Earlier that afternoon she had surprised me with a phone call; an impromptu business meeting with a regional curator (she's a very in-demand artist) had brought her into town for the night and she was hoping to see me. It had been well over two years since our last visit, so I was more than happy to abandon the tight routine of my life for the chance to spend a few hours with her.

Abby was the streak of red in my otherwise black-and-white world. She had been my roommate back in college, and in every way, my polar opposite. I would never forget the day she'd sailed through the door, a whirlwind of auburn curls and menthol cigarettes, and crashed into my orderly life. Abby had been the quintessential party girl, the one who never missed an opportunity to drink booze and fuck guys, or girls—she didn't care. She was an artist, a self-proclaimed free spirit, living her life in the same loud and vibrant colors she used to paint her canvases. Though she was a constant disruption to the quiet order I tried so hard to maintain, I loved her immediately. She had a warm irreverent smile that took my breath away every time I saw it. My mother would have considered her a bad influence, but I was magnetically drawn by her wild energy. I had never met anyone quite like her before and haven't since.

Back in those days, my academic career had been my first priority, and being the devout scholar I was, that meant sacrificing countless parties and dates on the altar of higher learning. I had been known as the nice girl, the one who always played by the rules. I did what was expected; it was something I prided myself on. I was good at being the good girl. It wasn't just a well-deserved reputation; it was my identity. At least that's what I thought, but being around Abby made the carefully controlled woman I believed myself to be come undone.

What no one ever knew was how cut off I felt, or the jealousy that would seep into my bones every time I heard the door close behind Abby's black stilettos. It was all I could do not to follow her clicking stride as she set off into the night. Never in my life had I felt so desperately alone. I tried not to think about where she was, or what she was doing, tried to keep my focus strictly on my studies, but my mind always wandered back to her. Sometimes she would be gone for days, and I would be half-mad with worry, but eventually she would come back, and when she did, she would sit on the edge of my bed recounting her X-rated adventures in lurid detail. Shrugging it off, I would feign disinterest, but secretly I wanted more. Every word she said set my imagination on fire.

My mind would swirl with visions of Abby down on all fours, her creamy freckled skin gleaming with sweat, her hazel eyes glossed over with lust. I could almost hear the primal sound of her moaning while getting gangbanged by a bunch of loud and rowdy frat boys, see their eager hands grabbing, slapping and pulling at her tits, their thick fingers buried in her flesh as they gripped her hips, each one taking his turn, pumping roughly into her juicy cunt. Even better was picturing Abby's red head buried between the shapely thighs of a drunken cheerleader lapping hungrily at the plump young pussy spread before her, sucking on the swollen clit and thrusting her little tongue, like a tiny dagger, as deep inside as it could go, devouring greedily, until her pretty face glistened with come. These images, like flames, burned brightly inside my mind, igniting a heat deep inside me that seemed to fill the room until I couldn't breathe.

Despite my indifference, Abby knew I savored those intimate stories. They were her way of making up for all the stress she caused me, but what she didn't realize was how I used those stories to keep myself company during my long and lonely nights of study-induced isolation. How easy it had been to recall the naughty glint behind her autumn eyes, and the sound of excitement twinkling in her voice as she relived her sexual conquests. Her words created my fantasies, filling my head to the brink, destroying my concentration until I couldn't help but touch myself. Daydreaming about Abby was my only relief. I would bring myself to orgasm over and over again, until my body was limp and shaking. The best thought of all, though, was wondering what Abby would do if she happened to walk in and catch me in the act. This fantasy was truly unbearable and always made me come the hardest.

"You're pretty quiet over there," Steve said, glancing at me with concern.

"Sorry," I replied. "Just have a lot on my mind."

"Thinking about the good old days?"

"Yeah," I chuckled. "Something like that." If only he knew.

By the time we arrived at the restaurant, I was already wet. She was there and waiting, sitting cross-legged at the bar in a typical Abby dress, too short and too tight, sipping on a lime margarita. Even in the dimly lit space I could see that time wasn't having much of an effect on her. Her beauty appeared virtually unchanged, perhaps a little more refined since the last time we had seen each other. Her in-your-face sex appeal had been polished into something a little more alluring and sophisticated, but still the air around her sparkled with the promise of sexual ecstasy.

"Cami!" she squealed, jumping down from her perch and bouncing over to embrace me tightly. "It's so good to see you!"

"It's good to see you, too, Abby," I laughed, holding on a little longer than I should have.

We walked together arm in arm as the hostess showed us to our table. Steve commented on being the envy of all the men in the restaurant as he pulled out our chairs; I couldn't help but notice the way his brown eyes never left her cleavage as he said it. I could hardly blame him; her body was a forbidden fruit, ripe with possibility.

It didn't take the two of us long to catch up, and by the time the first round of drinks had been served, it felt as if no time had passed between us at all. That's how it was with Abby; she always knew just how to speak to me, how to use the soft edges of her words, or the slight touch of her hand to draw me out of my shell. We laughed so hard our cheeks ached, and talked until the blazing sky outside had faded to black.

I wasn't sure if it was the sangria, or the magic of her presence, but somewhere over the course of the meal, I realized that our conversation had become flirtatious. It was only half-hearted at first, playful, like a dirty joke, or a compliment with a sensual twist, but along the way, between the appetizers and entrees, our words had begun to carry the weight of intention. My normally reserved inhibitions had become nothing more than a crumbling wall, letting loose a strange new idea which skittered nervously along the outskirts of my mind. I couldn't deny how much I wanted her; curiosity had burned inside me for so long, it had become a dull aching throb. I could never go behind my husband's back though; cheating was cheating, even with a woman, but if I had his permission…

I knew Steve wouldn't mind sharing me with another woman; he himself had said what a turn-on it would be. "What guy hasn't thought about being with two women?" he'd joked. Only one question remained; could I share my husband without jealousy ripping me apart?

The three of us together—the image flickered like a firefly behind my eyes. Just the very thought of it spread the rousing warmth of desire throughout my entire body, making my palms sweat and my hands tremble ever so slightly. I crossed and uncrossed my legs, enjoying the smooth silky feeling of freshly shaved skin, although doing so only seemed to stimulate the growing heat between my legs. I could tell similar thoughts were stirring in Abby based on the way she kept biting at her lower lip, a sexy little habit she'd had since college, and something she only did when sex was on her mind. I knew she'd always had a thing for Steve, admitting to me once how hot his tall and muscular frame made her, and how she wished she'd fucked more football players when she had the chance. I knew I could trust him, so I took it as a compliment. Maybe tonight she would have the opportunity, a little voice whispered in my head.

"I don't want this night to end," Abby sighed, gazing at me with her golden-green eyes. "I've missed you so much."

"Me, too," I agreed, holding her stare, hoping she could sense my hidden longing.

"I know," Steve interjected. "You're staying not too far from here, right, Abby? Why don't we buy a bottle or two of wine and head over for a nightcap?"

"Sounds good to me," she said, handing the waitress her credit card and flashing me that knowing smile I remembered all too well. Grinning to myself as we left the restaurant, I couldn't help but relish the sound of my own high heels clicking across the terra-cotta tiles. Tonight I was going to lead the way, consequences be damned.

Abby had booked a room in the historic district, just off the boulevard, in a quaint little bed-and-breakfast known as the Ava House. Complete with white shutters and a wraparound porch, it was a charming old house, with years of character in every nook and cranny. Abby never stayed in hotels when she traveled, claiming they were too conventional and generic. Instead she found places where she felt inspired, then used that inspiration later on in her paintings. We tiptoed like sneaky teenagers up the stairs to the top floor, the timeworn hardwood creaking under our feet as our muffled laughter filled the dark hallway.

Once safely in the room, I excused myself to the bathroom and faced the mirror. My outward reflection was calm, but beneath my smooth unruffled exterior, a potent combination of insecurity and excitement churned. I splashed cold water on my wine-flushed cheeks and scrutinized the woman framed in glass. Did I really have the guts to go through with my plan? This was something Abby would do, not me—not the good girl—yet, in that moment, I couldn't imagine doing anything else.

In the bedroom just beyond, I could hear Abby's laughter bubbling brightly as Steve lavished her with his charm. Her little crush was becoming more apparent with each glass of wine. I loved and trusted them both; who better to live out this fantasy with? Still, I worried, wondering if they would reject my advances. Not likely, I thought as I listened to their flirty banter. My anticipation intensified my desire. I needed this. A life lived vicariously through someone else was no life at all, even if that person was as outrageous and beautiful as Abby. Tonight I needed to live for myself, throw my worrisome what-ifs in the trash, and be the woman I had only dared be in my dreams. I reapplied my lipstick—dark red, the color of rebellion—and fluffed up my short blonde bob with a few small head flips before exiting.

"We were beginning to wonder if you fell in!" Steve laughed and handed me a fresh glass of wine. I sashayed over to him, accepting the proffered drink, and nestled down in his lap. I could feel his arousal through my skirt and made it a point to squirm more than usual. Sexual tension infused the air like smoke; it was in every look and every movement, emanating from our pores, but years of self-control and inexperience made navigating the situation difficult. I took a long sip of wine, letting the dry bitterness coat my throat, a shot of liquid courage. It was now or never. Seizing the moment, I made my move, leaning in toward Steve for a kiss.

I knew Steve would be expecting the standard married kiss, quick and modest, but little did he know that tonight I had no intention of being anything of the sort. I parted my lips, coaxing Steve's mouth open with my tongue, inviting him to stay awhile longer. Instinctively, he obliged, but kept himself properly restrained. When he finally did pull back, his eyes were wide and uncertain; it wasn't like me to show such public displays of affection. I bent forward again, this time holding his face firmly between my hands, keeping his mouth from escaping my own.

"What are you doing?" he whispered.

"Kissing you," I replied, careful to keep the rhythm going despite our bits of conversation.

"But what about Abby, darling? We don't want to make her feel uncomfortable."

I stopped then, looking at her directly. "You don't mind, do you sweetie?" A wicked smile uncoiled itself on my lips.

"Not at all," she answered back. Then, like a dare, added coyly, "You know I like to watch."

Picking up our kiss where it left off, I watched her watching me, the thrill of exhibition soaking my panties. I wanted her closer, and beckoned to her with my fingers. Accepting my invitation, Abby sauntered over, sitting down next to us on the couch, her eyes never leaving our mouths. Sitting so close I could see her pupils dilate, and knew the scene was turning her on. Much to my surprise, Steve made the next move. Tentatively, he reached out his hand and rested it atop her bare knee, caressing it with his thumb in slow circles, careful not to let his lips stray from mine.

Abby uncrossed her legs so they fell open slightly, allowing Steve's hand better access. Taking the hint, he began inching higher and higher up her tender inner thigh, and as I watched it rise, so did my desire. He stopped just below the hem of her dress, his hand shaking. He looked at me, his dark eyes desperate for my permission. Abby waited patiently. I was sure she expected my answer to be no. She didn't think I had the nerve, but I wasn't the same person she had known—not in this room, not tonight. I wasn't sure yet who I was becoming, but one thing was certain: I was no longer afraid. I stared at her boldly as I laid my hand over Steve's and guided it up the rest of the way, giving them both my wholehearted consent.

Abby whimpered softly as Steve's fingers made contact with her pussy. It didn't surprise me that she wasn't wearing any panties; she never had in college either. I couldn't believe the rush of fire between my legs at seeing my husband's fingers exploring Abby like that. I hesitated only slightly before taking the final plunge, pressing her full lips to mine. Her velvet mouth moved like a slow dance against my own, the faint trace of perfume from her lipstick lingering on my tongue. It was gentle, yet strangely familiar.

After a few shared kisses with Abby, I slid from Steve's lap and onto my knees. My hands worked fast to undo his pants, releasing his solid cock from its restraint. I was amazed at how hard and ready he already was. Eagerly, I took him into my mouth, moving my head up and down his length.

"Oh my god," Steve groaned.

I knew Abby was watching my naughty little performance, which only made me more intent on giving Steve the best blow job he'd ever had. I felt his hand on the back of my head, pushing his cock deeper down my throat, at the same time Abby's perfectly manicured fingers wrapped around its thick base and stroked it in perfect rhythm with my sucking. While Steve fucked my mouth, I listened to the wet sounds of him and Abby kissing and the quiet moans of pleasure flowing freely between her mouth and his. Her legs were open wide and I watched in awe as his fingers disappeared inside her. I saw the slickness of her pussy shimmering on Steve's fingers as he worked them in and out.

"Mmm," said Abby. "You make that look so good, Cami. Mind if I have a turn?"

I moved over, making room for her to kneel beside me, and she took over with a ferocity that quickly brought Steve to the edge. I devoured this scene with my eyes—my best friend sucking my husband's cock, him pumping into the soft center of her mouth and groaning like a wild animal. It was surreal, like the sensation of some faraway dream that would be forgotten in the morning.

"You've been wanting this all night, haven't you, Steve?" My words were more of a statement than a question.

"Fuck yeah," he grunted.

I kept waiting for the inevitable jealousy to come and rip through the moment, but it never did. Instead the fever between my legs only seemed to escalate. Abby's mascara began to run as she forced Steve's cock even deeper down her throat, the delicious sounds of her slurping and gagging my own personal aphrodisiac. I knew Steve wasn't going to last much longer. I wanted him to come—better yet, I wanted to see Abby make him come.

"Don't stop," I ordered, gripping Abby's hair with my fingers, pulling and pushing her head down on to Steve. "Suck his fucking cock, you slut," I heard myself say. "That's right, choke on it." I couldn't believe I was saying these things; my voice sounded unfamiliar, even to me. Steve's eyes widened in disbelief, but he was too close to coming to form any words. Abby groaned loudly; I knew from all her stories how much she liked dirty talk.

"Finish him off," I said. "I wanna see his come dripping off your chin."

"Holy shit," Steve growled, finally losing control. Just as I commanded, he shot his load all over Abby's waiting mouth.

While Steve regained his composure, Abby and I ripped at each other's clothes and moved closer to the bed. Although I'd seen her naked plenty of times during school, nothing could have prepared me for the vulnerability I felt standing naked in front of her. She looked at me and smiled, pearls of come still shining on her chest. Everywhere her eyes traveled left a trail of goose bumps on my skin. My heart was pounding against my ribs, so loud I was sure that she could hear it.

"You always did have the nicest tits," she said with admiration. "Since the day I met you I've wanted to know what they would feel like in my mouth. Why don't you feed them to me," she whispered.

Unable to deny her, I cupped my heavy breasts and brought them to her lips. Electricity blasted through every vein in my body as her tongue flickered lightly across my nipples. I whimpered helplessly, no longer in control of my actions. Raw instinct had taken over my body; it moved with a will of its own. I looked over at Steve; he was absorbed in the scene before him, a gnawing hunger growing in his eyes. It wouldn't be long before he'd be ready again.

Arching my back, I thrust my tits farther into her mouth, feeling like I could come standing there just like that. Not yet though; I pulled away. It was her turn first, and I wanted to own her. Bringing her mouth to mine, I tasted the salty tang of Steve's come on her lips. It tasted good, and I followed the sticky line, kissing her from her neck down the soft slope of her breast. A small metal barbell jutted through her left nipple. I took it between my teeth, tugging gently. I heard her sharp intake of breath and knew she was as close as I was. "Oh god," she breathed against my neck. Her tits filled my hands and then some, as soft as the inside of a shell.

"Lie down, Abby," I quietly demanded, "and spread your legs." She followed instructions well.

Gathering up her legs, I brought her hairless pussy within inches of my face. I opened her up with my tongue and lapped at her hot little opening. She was sweet and tart like a strawberry; I savored every last drop of her juice.

"You're driving me crazy," she panted, pulling my head in deeper.

My own pussy was slick and swollen, aching to be filled. My ass gyrated like I was fucking the air. Stroking my clit, I could feel my orgasm building deep within my core.

"Come in her face," Steve said as he plunged into me from behind. He bucked wildly, his staying power all but gone. As his cock stretched me in a painfully sweet way, I penetrated Abby with two fingers, thrusting them inside her the same way Steve's cock was thrusting into me. The force of his fucking pushed my face hard into the folds of her cunt, while she added to the intensity by grinding against my mouth. I nipped and sucked at her engorged clit, feeling it quiver under my tongue as she screamed her release.

I closed my eyes, my own orgasm ripping through me. Bursts of light and color exploded like a comet shooting across the sky. We roared together. Abby's pussy milked my fingers. I moaned with pleasure, imagining how good I was making Steve feel, too.

"Let me taste her," Steve said. I pulled out my fingers, coated in Abby's sweet syrup. I offered them to him to suck clean, then kissed him deeply, tasting all three of us at once.

We untangled and collapsed into a quivering heap of arms and legs. Moonlight filtered in through the blinds, casting a silver glow on our sweat-covered bodies.

"No fair," Abby pouted. "I never got to taste you."

"Maybe next time," I replied breathlessly, sated and empowered. Now that I knew what I'd been missing, next time couldn't come soon enough.

ORGANICALLY GROWN

Brandy Fox

When I got herpes from my husband and found out he was cheating on me, I kicked him out and took solace in the unlikeliest of places—our neighborhood natural food market. It fed me, both literally and figuratively. The rainbow of color in the produce section made my day feel brighter. The giant bins of granola and brown rice and whole-wheat flour assured me the world overflowed with possibility. I'd take a cold plunge by gliding through the freezer section, then dash to the deli to defrost by the rotisserie. The comfort of slow-cooked food, the pungent smell of bulk spices—a dizzying array of curry, basil, cayenne and ginger—and the knowledge that everything in the store was produced fairly and sustainably never failed to lull me into a state of pure bliss.

My five-year-old, Lily, loved it, too. But her reason was much simpler: she got a free piece of fruit on each visit. So we started grocery shopping every day. I probably should have been spending less time at the market and more time at GreenSingles. com. But after getting burned by my husband, I was paranoid about giving someone herpes or getting something even worse. Visiting the market every day and cooking up a fresh meal for Lily and me, then heading to bed with my dildo and a good collection of erotic stories, satisfied my every need.

And then the market hired a new produce guy.

There is something incredibly hot about a man in a vinyl apron handling organic fruit and vegetables. When that man has a smile so bright it could power a grow light and hemp jeans that hug tight glutes, it's easy to find excuses to return to the produce section multiple times in one trip. Within a couple weeks, we were on a first-name basis with Frank the Hot Produce Guy.

One day I wore a black T-shirt made of organic cotton that wrapped like iceberg lettuce around my melon-sized breasts, with a low-cut V-neck that dipped low on my cleavage. I paired it with a colorful pendant and butt-hugging low-rider jeans for another trip to the grocery store, where Lily got a piece of free fruit and I got a free peek at Frank.

When the automatic doors parted to let us in, he was sorting fruit near the entrance. He greeted us with that electric smile. His gaze flicked down to my chest, then back to the peaches cupped in his hands.

"Free fruit!" my daughter shouted from the cart.

"What would you like today, Lily? Peaches? Strawberries?" Frank teased, because Lily always asked for an apple. "How about a banana?"

I'd like your banana.

As if he'd heard my dirty thoughts, his emerald eyes met mine. Was it my imagination, or was he blushing? I gripped the cart handle, trying to calm my racing pulse.

"Apple!" Lily shouted.

I wheeled the cart to the apples and let my hands linger over their smooth green skins before choosing one and handing it to Frank. As he took it, our fingers brushed, sending a charge through my abdomen. Now I was the one turning red.

When he returned with a cup of apple wedges, I thanked him. His eyes trailed down my clavicle to my pendant, then paused at my tits before coming up for air at my face. "Anytime, Gayle," he said with a husky voice that made the back of my neck sweat.

Reluctantly, I headed toward the dairy section for bulk eggs. Lily was too busy munching on apples to bother climbing out, so I parked the cart and grabbed my empty egg carton. With one knee, I propped the door open and bent down to choose the eggs one at a time. The brisk air cooled my flushed face and chest. I bent lower to let the air tease at my nipples. Movement in the back where stockers lurk to refill the dairy section made me look up. There, beyond the shelves of milk, those emerald eyes were staring.

I followed his gaze to my chest. What little was hidden underneath my T-shirt was all revealed now: the black bra, scooped down to show my taut nipples.

I gasped. The egg in my hand slipped and splattered on the floor near my feet.

"Oops, Mommy!" Lily shouted from the cart.

Instantly, Frank was by my side with a roll of paper towels. "I'll get that," he said, kneeling so that his pants tightened around his firm legs.

"I am so sorry!" I said, although I didn't feel entirely responsible for the mess. I knelt down and held out my hand for some towels to help clean up.

He glanced at my hand, my chest, then the floor. "No

problem. It's not your fault." He smiled mischievously.

"Yes, it is." Lily corrected him. "Mommy dropped the egg."

Frank swiped the floor one last time with a clean paper towel. "Well, yes. She did drop the egg." His eyes wandered once again to my cleavage, then up to my eyes. "Do you still need more?" he asked, holding his hand out for the egg carton.

I gladly handed him the carton and watched his ass flex as he bent down. Cold air escaped around us and I imagined taking one of those eggs, crushing it against his asscheek and smearing it down his crack, around his balls and up his cock.

Abruptly, he turned around. "There you go." He handed me the carton and eyed my flushed face.

As I wheeled the cart away, Lily said, "Mommy, you look sick."

"I might be a little feverish," I replied. "We better get going."

I thought about Frank all the way home, my crotch twitching with the memory of his eyes on my bared breasts. I also noticed he didn't wear a wedding ring; I could ask him out. But the divorce was still so fresh, and the idea of juggling dates with single motherhood seemed daunting. First impressions and commitments and worrying about STDs and pregnancy—I just didn't have the energy for all that. What I did want—craved!— was safe sex with no strings attached. Was that even possible?

At home, I put away the groceries and set Lily in front of "Sesame Street." Claiming I needed to rest due to that fever, I went straight to my bedroom and pulled out my dildo.

In front of the full-length mirror, I stepped out of my jeans, spread my legs and lifted my shirt. I imagined the mirror to be the glass door between customers and the refrigerated section in the market, with Frank just beyond it, trapped behind the shelves of milk, watching me. He's in nothing but his apron, holding it aside to grasp his hard shaft. I'm leaning back on a pile of tomatoes, mushing them into my backside so their warm juices drip down my inner thighs. He watches me lick my fingers and squirrel them under my G-string to massage the juice into my labia. With my other hand, I pull aside my bra and pinch my nipple. I sway my hips, pressing them into my fingers, working my clit into a knot of fire. His cock stings with cold as he works it between two milk jugs. Then I squat on the ground, insert the dildo and imagine him overwhelmed with the need to crash through the glass door and thrust his cock deep inside me. But he can only watch as I writhe over that dildo and fondle my nipples. I imagined both of us throwing back our heads, mouths open wide as we screamed in a simultaneous climax.

After coming, I sank to the floor and let my fingers linger on my groin and nipples. I added up the days until Lily would be at her dad's house and I could grocery shop alone. Then I made a plan.

I put on nothing but a skirt and that same black T-shirt and returned during the slowest time of day. When I walked through the automatic doors, Frank was in his usual spot, shelving fruit and flashing his brilliant smile. "Hello, Gayle. No Lily today?"

"She's at her dad's house. Besides, there are certain errands I prefer to do alone." I smiled deceptively and headed for the tomatoes and garlic.

From behind me, Frank asked, "Planning something delicious for dinner?" He was so close I could smell his woodsy cologne.

"I was thinking about a fresh marinara sauce."

"Perfect day for it. Tomatoes were picked yesterday." He picked up a hothouse tomato, tossed it into his other hand and lifted it toward the light on the tips of his fingers like a trophy. "Firm yet juicy." His glance fell to my cleavage, then quickly back to the tomato. "Holds up in heat," he continued. "Sautéed with a bit of olive oil and garlic, this tomato will be ecstasy on your tongue." We both struggled against a smile.

"But it's lost its stem," I pointed out. "Doesn't that mean its integrity has been compromised?"

He let the tomato drop into his palm. "You are absolutely right." He tossed it aside like trash and let his hand hover over the rack of tomatoes, as though sensing their energy. He homed in on a pair, hooked his finger around the bright green stem joining the two, and lifted it. "Now these are perfect."

I studied their undersides and declared, "One of them has a bruised bottom."

He slapped his hand on his forehead. "Young lady, you are a tough sell."

I chuckled at the "young lady" comment and glanced around at all the tomatoes. "I don't know," I said, shaking my head. "I'm planning to make a lot. There don't seem to be enough perfect ones here for an entire sauce. Is this all you have?"

His sharp emerald eyes met mine. "As a matter of fact," he said, wagging a finger, "we have another box in back. Would you like me to...choose some for you?" His eyes swept down the length of my body. "Or better yet..."

"Could I possibly—"

"Come see them?"

"For myself?" I gazed longingly at him.

His eyes twinkled with understanding. He glanced around at the produce section. There was one other customer stuffing a bunch of broccoli into a plastic bag, looking to be in a hurry.

"Of course you can. Come this way." He led me down the

aisle and through the same doorway he always disappeared into when cutting up Lily's apple. As I watched his ass muscles flex inside those tight hemp jeans, my pulse quickened. Was I really brave enough to do this?

I followed him around the corner and into a cool storage room with boxes of vegetables lined up on a counter. My breath caught with the sudden drop in temperature. He began looking through the boxes. Did he really think I was back here for tomatoes?

"Aha!" He came up with a perfect tomato. "These haven't been over-handled like the ones on the floor. I'm sure you'll find what you're looking for here."

I crossed my arms and leaned against the door frame. "I think I found exactly what I'm looking for." My gaze wandered to his bulge and lingered there for so long it grew right before my eyes.

The hand holding the tomato dropped to his side. He cleared his throat. "I don't think I…"

I approached him, stopping a couple inches away. Even in the cold room, the heat between us rose. I locked eyes with him and smiled knowingly. Then I caught sight of something behind him: a box of cucumbers. I reached around, took out the largest one I could find and held it up between us. "This is a gorgeous cucumber," I purred. "Have you ever experienced anything like it before?"

His Adam's apple twitched. "No, I don't believe I have."

I slowly stroked the whole length of the cucumber with two fingers, up and down. "Neither have I."

Frank rested his elbows on the counter behind him and leaned back, bending his knee up slightly. Was he backing away from my advances or trying to make me hotter? Now his vinyl-covered thigh stuck out like an invitation to my clit.

I took another step to close the gap between us, hiked up my skirt and pressed my bare, wet pussy into his cold, plastic-sheathed quad. Then I placed the cucumber between my breasts. "I believe you owe me one for the accident with that egg the other day."

His eyebrows rose in surprise. Finally he said, "I believe you're right." He reached his hand around to my ass and squeezed it, pressing my clit farther into his leg.

I tilted my head back in ecstasy and moaned, grinding into his thigh and rubbing my leg against his bulge. His other hand found my ripe breast and held it as gently yet firmly as he had the tomatoes. "Oh Gayle," he whimpered. "I bet you are delicious."

The cucumber seemed to throb in my hand. I pressed it between his pecs. With its tiny nub of a stem as hard as my nipples, I drew a line up the side of his neck, across his cheek and to his lips. "Lick it," I commanded. He flicked his tongue gingerly around its stem, then licked more voraciously across its wide, round bottom. His fingers seemed to move in unison across my breast—a flick of the nipple, then a wide sweep over its curves. With my free hand I combed his curly brown hair. Our thighs, his tongue, our groins and hands all moved to the rhythm of our moans until my pussy was aching for something hard and slick.

I stepped back from his thigh and rested a foot on the knee-high shelf under the table. I drew the cucumber down his neck, along his vinyl-covered chest and belly, finally reaching the length of his bulge straining under the apron. I pressed it against his cock, teasing. He pressed back.

Frank looked up at the doorway, then, apparently convinced we were safe, began pulling his apron aside. With the cucumber I slapped his hand away and declared, "That's staying put."

Then in one quick move, I dove the cucumber into the tent of my skirt. The moment its tip touched my drenched pussy, it yawned wide and welcomed it inside. The green, slick skin slid in and stretched me so wide I gasped.

Hastily, Frank ducked under my propped-up leg and came around back, leaving a wide-open space for me to thrust the cucumber in and out. I felt his throbbing cock, still safe inside his pants and apron, press between my buttocks. He grabbed my waist with both hands and pulled me against him. We quickly found a rhythm, his cock pressing into my ass just as the cucumber slid so deep inside me I imagined the two kissing at the small of my back.

After just a few kisses, the wave of an orgasm began at that point and swept down my ass, around my groin and into my belly. The moment it hit my throat and I began to yell, Frank clamped his hand over my mouth. A moment later, he had to stifle his own moan. Our grinding slowed to a small, sweet rhythm until I reluctantly pulled out the cucumber and placed it on the counter.

Frank laid his body across the length of my back, wrapped his arms around me and sighed. Then he reached into a box and withdrew a tomato. "Does this one satisfy your needs?"

I turned around to face him. "Absolutely. I'd like a dozen more just like it."

"And perhaps some cucumbers for a salad?"

I laughed. "And tomorrow I'll need something to eat with the leftover marinara sauce."

His eyes sparkled with mischief. "I believe I'll be shelving a shipment of sausage in the meat freezer."

The Room of Guarantees

Jessica Lennox

My first thought as I arrived at the door was *I can't believe I'm doing this.* On the other hand, I *could* believe it. I'd wanted this forever. My failed attempts at getting my partner to do anything kinky with me (including accompanying me to this club) had been particularly frustrating, and now that I was single again, I was ready to explore! I'd made several tentative visits already, but this time I was determined to have the full experience.

Upon entering the club, I showed the hottie security guard/doorperson my identification and handed over a twenty. Hottie looked down at my ID, smiled and then handed it back to me. I took it from her and tossed it into the depths of my handbag as I made my way toward the lounge. As my eyes adjusted to the dimmed lighting, I looked for a pathway to the bar, and secretly prayed for an available stool to sit on. I spotted one at the far end, and then felt like I was in one of those bad dreams where you feel like you're moving, but not getting any closer to whatever it is you're trying to reach. I felt as if I'd been walking through the lounge forever, with every pair of eyes on me, but then thankfully the nightmare ended, and I let out a sigh of relief as I reached my destination.

I sat down on the bar stool and took a few deliberate slow breaths before finally allowing myself to look around. From the outside, the club doesn't look any different than a dozen others in the neighborhood, neglected and sad, but inside, this club is like no other. This particular club caters to women and their appetites, whatever they may be. Drinking, dancing, voyeurism, exhibitionism, porn, cruising, bondage—you name it, you can find it here. Women everywhere, their attire ranging from various stages of nudity to fully dressed, from the finest leather chaps and boots, to the shortest chain-mail dresses and miniskirts—it's quite a sight.

I wanted to look around some more but decided a drink was definitely in order. I signaled with my hand for a bartender and ordered a vodka cranberry. As I waited for it, I turned around on my stool and scanned the room. It was a turn-on just to watch everyone—so many women, fine leather hugging their bodies, toys and other assorted devices hanging from belt loops. I was squirming in my seat by the time the bartender returned with my drink, took my money and made change all in one move. I took a long, slow sip as my eyes traveled toward the entryway. I think I stopped breathing for a moment as my eyes zeroed in on the hottest butch I'd seen yet. Dressed in motorcycle wear, with an attitude that radiated across the room, my newest obsession acted like she owned the place. Hell, for all I knew, maybe she did.

I watched every step of her journey as she navigated the maze of furniture and people and said hello to a dozen or more of them, kissing several girls on the cheek as she made her way through the crowd. As she walked past, she surprised me by stopping short and sliding right up to the bar between me and the woman sitting next to me. I didn't turn. I didn't blink. I don't know if I even took a breath. I glanced sideways at her without moving as she looked toward the end of the bar where both bartenders were pouring drinks. She shrugged to herself, and then turned and looked right at me. I swallowed so hard I was convinced she heard me. I looked at her then, and she smiled. I felt a twinge between my thighs. Apparently my body wasn't as nervous as my brain.

"You here alone?" she asked, looking me up and down.

"Yes," I said, rather abruptly, from nerves, but it sounded like I had an attitude.

She leaned forward and whispered in my ear, "Does your tone mean you don't like me and I should leave you alone? Or does it mean you're just nervous, and I should continue? I think you want me to continue, but I'll give you the benefit of answering."

I wasn't sure if I liked her cocky attitude. Oh, who was I kidding? I *loved* her cocky attitude, but I didn't know if I wanted her to know that. I took a breath, and then slowly turned toward her. "I *was* slightly nervous, but I'm feeling more at ease by the minute," I said, my voice shaking, betraying the false confidence I was trying so hard to convey.

She raised her eyebrow and said, "*Are* you now? Well, I'll take that as a sign to continue then." She leaned in so that her mouth was practically touching my earlobe, and for a moment she didn't say or do anything. My stomach jumped in anticipation, and finally she asked, "So, are you here alone? Meeting someone? Or are you planning to visit the Room tonight?"

Ah yes, the Room of Guarantees, or as the regulars call it, the Room. It's a cluster of rooms actually, all private, paid for by the hour—well, forty-five minutes, to be exact. I think the name was meant to be a joke, originally, but its reputation had lived up to its name; so far it hadn't yielded a single unsatisfied customer. For as little as a hundred bucks, you could engage in a variety of "therapeutic" acts with a paid professional.

As I tried to formulate a response to her question, I could feel the heat rising in my face. "Well, to be completely honest, I didn't have any plans set in concrete. But I did bring cash, just in case," I said, feeling nervous and determined all at the same time.

The raised eyebrow was back; apparently my answer amused her. "Well," she said, then glanced at her watch. "Oh, hey, I gotta go!"

"Wha—?" I started to ask, hearing that screeching halt sound in my head as my brain tried to process what was happening.

"It's not you. In fact, I'd like to spend more time with you..."

"Elise," I offered.

"...Elise. But my shift is about to start, and I have to get ready," she explained with a devilish grin.

"Oh!" I said with a start. "You...you work in the Room?" My voice squeaked on that last part.

"Yep," she said, flashing me a cocky smile. "Maybe you'll set those plans in concrete and come see me tonight, huh? I'd like to see you, and that isn't a professional come-on; I really mean it. You can ask for me at the desk; they call me Mick."

I didn't move or speak for what seemed like an eternity, and then finally gave myself a mental shove and said, "Okay, I'll give it some thought."

"You do that," Mick said, winking at me before she turned to walk away.

I watched her negotiate her way through the crowd, then through the black curtains that separated the Room from the rest of the club. As I downed the remainder of my drink, I considered paying her a visit (no pun intended). There had definitely been chemistry between us, and I believed it when she said it wasn't a professional come-on, and that she wanted to see me—or maybe I just wanted to believe her. I definitely wanted to see her, but now my options were limited to paying to see her, or waiting after hours in hopes of catching her before she left, or coming here again in the hopes of bumping into her. I didn't like the odds, so I went with my best bet: a paid visit.

I had never been to the Room before, but I had been intrigued by it since I had learned of its existence. I had peered through the curtains once, during one of my previous visits to the club, so this time, when I parted the curtains and stepped through them, I knew what to expect. After taking a deep breath, I stepped up to the check-in desk and nervously took a form from the stack on display. I didn't have any particular fantasy in mind, I only knew there was definite chemistry between Mick and myself, and I wanted her. I filled out the form, check-marking what seemed like a million boxes for things I did and didn't want or like, and my experience level, which of course was "novice" for the most part. Sure, I'd been spanked a few times, and I'd read a ton of books on BDSM, but for all intents and purposes, I was a novice. There was so much I wanted to explore eventually, but tonight, I really just wanted to be controlled.

With my completed form in hand, I stepped up and asked the clerk for the next available slot with Mick. I handed the paper to her and she fed it into a scanner, and then made a few taps on her keyboard while she read the information on the screen. After a few clicks of her mouse she said, "Pretty much whenever you want except for eleven to midnight; that spot's blocked out."

I looked at my watch: nine-fifty. "Can I have ten o'clock?"

"Sure, sweetie. That'll be one hundred dollars for ten o'clock to ten-forty-five," she said as she started clicking and tapping again. A few seconds later she said, "Okay, Elise," referring to the form for my name. "Any room preference?"

"No," I replied, butterflies taking flight in my stomach, "no room preference."

"Great, then you're all set," she said with a smile. "Here's your receipt and your door tag. Please place the tag on the outside of the door; the receipt is yours to keep. You'll be in the Mod Room. You can go on back now, the room is ready, and your session will start in about ten minutes."

"Thank you," I said, my hand shaking as I took the receipt and the door tag, which simply had OCCUPIED painted on it in pink neon. I walked toward the archway that led to the rooms, showing my door tag to the bouncer, who looked at it and then motioned for me to proceed down the hallway. As I walked, I looked at each door with its artfully painted room name, and finally arrived at the end of the hall. The last room on the left sported a placard with THE MOD ROOM in black and white letters.

I opened the door slowly, peeked inside and then placed the door tag on the outside knob. As I stepped inside, I couldn't help but notice the décor. Everything was done in black-and-white, retro '60s style. The bedspread was actually making me dizzy with its swirls and mismatched pillows. It was distracting enough that at first I didn't notice the eyebolts in the headboard, and in the wall above and on either side of it. I turned to survey the rest of the room and admired the floor to ceiling mirror with a ballerina bar. That could be interesting. Other than that, the room was relatively standard with one upholstered chair, and a small, black-and-white-checkered bathroom.

I glanced at the clock and realized my session was going to start in about three minutes. Since I hadn't listed any particular fantasy, I realized that I had no idea how this was going to go. But frankly, I didn't care that much; I just wanted to explore something new and enjoy myself. Not to mention, Mick was hot! Not only did I not want to waste a single minute once she got here, I wanted her to want me. Although I hadn't planned my night completely, I knew I wanted something to happen, and I had dressed for the occasion. I stripped out of my short skirt and sheer blouse with the plunging neckline, and left only my lingerie and heels on. I walked toward the mirror and gave my reflection the once-over as I straightened the laces of my corset. I had to admit, I looked damn good—sexy, even. I straightened my stockings and was fiddling with my hair when Mick entered the room.

"Yes, you're hot," she said, her voice startling me. I turned to greet her but she quickly said, "No, don't turn around. Stay just like that, facing the mirror. Put your hands on the bar and close your eyes."

I complied without reservation. It was easy to trust her, I don't know why. I guess part of it was knowing that she was a professional, employed by the club—not some random stranger who might disappear off the face of the planet after murdering me. Also, the club had a spotless reputation; I'd never heard of anything bad happening here. But most of all, I wanted to trust her. I wanted to give in to her and lose myself in the moment.

With my eyes closed, my other senses became heightened. I could hear her footsteps as she approached the spot where I stood. I could feel how close she was standing even before she touched me. She ran her fingers down my arms, causing goose bumps to appear everywhere on my body. "Keep your eyes closed and concentrate on how my hands feel on your skin," she whispered. I swallowed hard, gripping the bar in front of me and squeezing my eyes shut even tighter. "You look so beautiful like this," she said as she swept my hair away from my neck, causing me to shiver. When she started sucking on my neck, I moaned and let go of the bar to reach behind me.

"No, don't let go of the bar," she said, in a commanding voice. "If I have to tell you again, I'll cuff you to it, under-stand?"

I nodded, placing my hands back on the bar and keeping my eyes closed.

"That's a good girl, stay just like that," she said, continuing to lick and kiss her way down my neck and between my shoulder blades. I felt one of her boots slide between my feet and gently nudge them apart. I was so aroused I could feel my juices soaking the crotch of my panties already. Her hands were in my hair, pulling my head back, keeping my neck exposed. She gave a quick tug on my hair, and I moaned out loud.

"You like that. Good. There's more where that came from," she said, pulling my hair sharply to the side as she bit my shoulder. The pain of it was shocking at first, but quickly overshadowed by sexual arousal. She kept nipping at my neck as her hands reached in and scooped my breasts out of my corset. I felt my nipples instantly harden, and heat flushed my face. Suddenly everything stopped. I wanted to open my eyes, but I felt compelled to obey her directive to keep them shut. I knew that Mick was still standing behind me because I could hear her breathing, but she wasn't touching me, or saying anything. Even though I couldn't be sure, I sensed she was staring at my breasts in the mirror. Whether that was from my heightened senses, or my mind going into hyperdrive from the silence and lack of physical contact, I felt more and more self-conscious as the seconds ticked away.

Just when I didn't think I could stand it anymore, I felt Mick's fingertips slowly circle around each nipple, carefully avoiding any direct contact with them. It felt wonderful for the first minute or so, but all I wanted was for her to touch them, pinch them, anything. I felt like I was going to scream if she didn't stop teasing me soon, and I whimpered in frustration. Slowly, slowly, all around, her fingertips kept traveling, and then finally she clamped both nipples between her fingers and squeezed.

"Oh, thank you," I moaned. Those words surprised me. I didn't realize how grateful I felt until those words escaped my mouth.

"Open your eyes," she commanded.

I slowly opened my eyes and looked at both of us in the mirror. The look on my face was pure ecstasy, and I was glad to see that the look on hers was pure lust.

"I want you to watch as I play with you," she said. I watched in the mirror as she pulled the fabric of my panties aside with one hand and began gently stroking my swollen sex with the other. I continued to hold on to the ballet bar, but slumped against her as I watched her play with me. I was mesmerized by her fingers, the tips wet with my juices. I was starting to feel almost hypnotized when suddenly she surprised me by plunging two fingers deep inside me. I gasped at the suddenness of it, but it felt so good, I began pushing against her, clamping down on her fingers.

"Look at your face, Elise. Look at how excited you are," she panted.

I tore my eyes away from her hand and forced myself to look straight forward. I looked hot and lustful.

"You like watching me play with your pussy? Mmm...you're nice and wet, just like I knew you'd be. I can't wait to fuck you with my cock." I sucked my breath in sharply as she pushed her hips forward, her hard bulge suddenly pressing against my ass. I don't know why it hadn't occurred to me that she might be packing, but I was oh so thankful to learn that she was. I pushed back, rubbing against her crotch.

"Oh, you like that, do you? That's good to know, because I am going to fuck you like you deserve to be fucked. That's what you came here for, isn't it? Well, isn't it?" she asked, more forcefully, taking a handful of my hair in her fist and pulling my head back.

"Yes," I whispered, feeling aroused, yet shamefully exposed at the same time.

She let go of my hair and spun me around. "Down on your knees, pretty girl."

I slid down without hesitation, looking up at her, sensing what was coming next and practically salivating at the idea of it. The wicked grin on her face told me I was right.

"You've guessed what comes next, haven't you?" she asked

as she slowly took her cock out and revealed it to me. "Well, open up that pretty mouth then. I know you want it, I can see it in your eyes."

I opened my mouth just enough to stick my tongue out and lick all around the head of her cock. She moaned, and my clit twitched from the sound of it. I continued to lick, slurp and kiss her cock up and down the length of the shaft, and then finally, I took the entire length into my mouth.

"Holy fuck," she hissed as she put her hands behind my head and alternated between stroking my hair and grabbing it in her hands. I moaned as I sucked her off, moving my head back and forth, using my hands to jack her off at the same time.

I felt her hands tighten in my hair when she suddenly said, "Stop. Stop! I want to come while I'm fucking you. Turn around and lean forward with your elbows on the bar. Now watch yourself while I fuck you." And with that, she tore my panties aside and buried herself to the hilt in my cunt.

Something that sounded like a cat in heat escaped my lips as I took the full length of her cock. "Fuck," I gasped as she pounded into me. I was holding on to the bar, bracing myself against it, taking everything she was giving me. "Oh, god," I cried, "please don't stop!"

"I'm not gonna stop," she reassured me. "Look at how beautiful you are, impaled on my cock. I could fuck you like this all night, Elise. Do you want me to fuck you all night?"

Of course I did, but even though I was at the height of ecstasy, my brain suddenly clicked on, and I wondered how much time we had left. I was tempted to look at the clock, but I forced myself out of my head and simply answered, "Yessss" through gritted teeth.

"Damn, you're hot, girl," Mick growled in my ear as she

ground into me. "I wanted to fuck you the moment I saw you tonight. And now here I am, my cock buried deep in your luscious pussy. I don't think life can get any better than this."

The sound of her voice in my ear was too much. Her words, so deliciously nasty, spurred me toward a mind-blowing orgasm. "Don't stop," I hissed, "I'm almost there."

She started thrusting harder. "Good, I want you to come for me. I can feel your tight pussy gripping me, coaxing my cock to come inside you. You want me to come inside you, don't you? Come on, Elise, we're both right there, now come for me!"

I did exactly as she commanded—I came so hard I thought I was going to lose my mind. I could feel the muscles of my cunt pulsing around her cock, and I swear her cock was alive inside me. She held me against her as she thrust into me and growled in my ear, then finally with one long, drawn-out moan she brought us both collapsing to the floor.

After a few minutes, I opened my eyes and looked up at her. "We have to leave now, don't we? I suppose your next appointment is starting soon." I couldn't keep the disappointment from creeping into my voice. I didn't want to sound needy but I really wanted nothing more than to stay with her.

"Nope, we have at least another hour, if not longer," she said, kissing me on the forehead and stroking my hair.

"Are you sure? When I booked this appointment, the desk clerk said you were blocked out from eleven to midnight."

"I am. I blocked it out myself so I could go back to the bar and talk to you if you were still around. So basically, I'm free for at least another hour. Hang on a second."

She disentangled herself and made her way over to the nightstand, then dialed the phone as I stood up to gather my clothes.

"Yeah, Sue, this is Mick," I heard her say into the phone. "Do I have any other appointments booked for later tonight? Okay, go ahead and block me out. I'm busy the rest of the night, thanks."

I spun around as she hung up the phone. "Does this mean...?"

"Yep. I'm all yours, if you want me," she said as she led me toward the bed. "Free of charge, of course."

REDRAWING THE LINES

Bren Emile

$\mathcal{A}$re you sure about this?" They're nearing the point of no return, and the palm she has wrapped around the crop's handle is sweaty.

He rolls his eyes at her. "Yes. And just so you know, the next time you ask? My answer is still going to be yes. Just like it was the last three times." He shifts on the bed, moving into as comfortable a position as he can manage. She resettles herself, sitting astride his narrow hips, staring down at him. She's wearing her black lace panties and a red bra; both are favorites of Brandon's. She's got her hair down; it tumbles in tangles down her back. She knows that he likes her hair; he's told her that he likes feeling it slide through his fingers, likes tugging on it as if they were back in kindergarten when love was as simple as a pulled pigtail.

He can't tug on her hair now; she let it down just to tease him.

He can't tug on it now, because she's tied his hands and legs to the corners of the bed and strapped him tight.

Their double bed is old, but at least it doesn't creak. They bought the under-the-bed bondage straps two weeks before and they've been tucked away in her closet since then, like a Christmas present waiting to be unwrapped. Her lace panties rub against the hard line of his cock when she shifts her hips. It's obvious he's enjoying this—enjoying the view, enjoying the sensation, enjoying the anticipation. Her own enjoyment is tinged with apprehension. She's probably more afraid than he is. She adjusts her grip on the riding crop. It's brand new; she'd taken the tag off right before climbing on the bed. She runs it through the fingers of her free hand. Brandon's wide eyes follow her movements. She watches his Adam's apple bob as he swallows.

"Ready?" she asks. He nods.

She's nervous the first time she hits him. She worried about the angle and the force and the timing, but when his body jolts underneath her—an involuntary reaction to pain—her cunt clenches. There is something automatic in her pleasure, something instinctual in her response. An ache she's never felt before has settled itself inside of her.

"How did it feel?" She hadn't hit hard enough to leave a mark, but she hadn't expected to yet. On their one-year anniversary, he'd asked her to leave a hickey on him, and she'd sucked on his collarbone until she felt like a vampire, just to give him a mark that would last longer than a day. His eyes are open wide and she thinks that if she bites him now, hard, it would leave a deeper, lasting bruise; she wonders how hard she'd have to hit him so that the marks will be there when the sun rises.

"You already know how it feels," he says. And he's right, she does know, kind of. She'd tried the crop on herself in the store and again at home, learning the feel of it, adjusting the force. But theory is one thing; the two of them actually playing this out is different. She slaps him again and this time she leaves a line that almost lands over his nipple. When her aim improves, that's where she's going to concentrate the pain.

"Did I ask you how *I* felt?"

He opens his mouth, then closes it again. She holds herself very still. Because it's not about the crop, not really; it's not about the black leather of the handle or the graceful way it curves at the end; it's not about the handcuffs on his wrists or the lingerie that makes her feel desirable and strong.

"No," he says, then adds, "Ma'am." She bites back a gasp. She wants to call him a good boy, *her* good boy, but in the silence that fills the space between them, with the air echoing from her crop slapping his skin and his low voice, she doesn't know if it would sound right.

"How did it feel to *you*?" she asks again.

He doesn't respond until she raises the crop again. "I don't know," he says hastily. "It hurt? But not that badly, I guess; it was more of a surprise than anything. You can hit me harder. Swing it like you swing a flyswatter. That's what the guy at the store said. Just—"

She's tired of listening to him talk. She's tired of his answers, which he always stretches out too long. She's tired of letting him set the pace of their conversations, tired of him talking to her like he's the benevolent teacher and she the constant pupil. She's tired but underneath that familiar, humble fatigue, there's a new kind of fire. She takes a good look at him—his handsome face, the stretched-out muscles of his long, tan arms—and hits him again. And then again. *That's four strikes*, she thinks, as she grinds against his hard cock. She hits his left nipple with the fifth hit, and then hits it again and again until he starts swearing.

"If you want me to stop," she says, "then say 'red.'" Her voice is sweet and strange as she drags the crop in a line from his neck to his navel. She feels like some other woman—some ancient queen of old—has taken over her body and mind and heart and is using it in the way she's always wanted to. She traces the crop up her torso, from her oversensitive clit to her hardened nipples. She feels more comfortable in her own body than she can ever remember being. She feels proud of the faint stretch marks on her breasts and her off-center nose, proud of her teeth and scars. She smiles and loves the wrinkles that are beginning to show around the corners of her eyes.

Underneath her, her beautiful boyfriend is gasping for breath. Red patches are beginning to show on his chest. She lets him catch his breath, watching his rib cage expand. Eventually she realizes he's not going to ask her to stop. "Good boy," she says, suddenly breathless herself, suddenly in control of the silence. "Say 'thank you' if you want me to keep going."

It takes him a few seconds to work up the courage to say it. His jaw clenches, his lips going white with tension, before he lets the words out. "Thank you," he says, and then a second later, as if the word's a surprise to him as well, he adds, "Ma'am."

She shuffles backward on the bed and then straddles his right thigh, his muscles shaking underneath her. It's not as sexy as before, she knows, but this way she can ride him, finally get the friction on her clit that she's been craving for hours. And this way she gets more leverage. The red line springs up right away when she hits him this time. He swears, then bites his lip and says, "Sorry." With the next couple of blows he stays quiet and she realizes that she doesn't like the silence as much as she'd enjoyed the way Brandon responded to every hit, like a call-and-response Greek chorus, a hard slap followed by his breathless cursing. With his sounds contained like this she feels disconnected from him.

"Make noise," she says. "Okay? Brandon?" He nods, making eye contact with her, which he doesn't break even when she starts in on his right nipple. She feels invincible, like an Amazon. When her arm begins to feel sore (she is going to cover his entire chest before she stops, his chest and his thighs will be red and sore and raw because of *her*) she takes a break. She reaches behind herself and undoes the clasp of her bra with one hand. He moans when she slides the straps from her shoulders, and for the first time he begins to struggle with his bonds.

"What would you do to me if you could touch me?" she asks honestly, idly curious.

"Oh *god*," he says, throwing his head back against the cushion. "I'd—I'd touch you all over."

"Be more specific."

"Your breasts," he says; she can almost hear him rolling his eyes. "You know that already." She moves farther down the bed and lays a flurry of strikes across his belly, careful not to hit his cock. (Yet.) "Your nipples," he hisses through clenched teeth. "I'd trace them with my tongue and when they were wet I'd pinch them. Get them hard before I'd start working them with my teeth."

"Open up." She holds her left hand over his mouth and slips two fingers in when he obeys, caressing his tongue and brushing across his bottom lip. Then she drags the spit-slick fingers up her torso and starts drawing circles around her nipples, the circles getting smaller and smaller until she's just rubbing the nub between her fingertips.

Usually, she doesn't get off on this; she likes her breasts played with, but has never gotten much out of it when going solo. *Maybe it's not what I'm doing*, she thinks. *Maybe it's what it's doing to Brandon.* She squeezes her left nipple between her fingertips and pinches as hard as she can every time she swings the crop. She moves her whole torso when she swings; she's never been into sports, but now she wants to learn how to play tennis, baseball, cricket, wants her body to learn this intimately. Her breasts shift but she keeps her left hand still, the pain in her nipple an added thrill. Brandon watches her breasts move, watches her nipple distend, watches her breast stretch in the fraction of a moment right before the crop lands.

Eventually her arms begin to tire. She gets off the bed to remove her panties, cursing when they tangle around her ankles. She stops before she gets back on the bed and just looks at him, looks at the tension in his limbs and the sweat dampening his hair and the red blossoming under his skin. "I could leave you like this," she whispers. She could leave him hard and ready and begging for as long as she wanted to. Minutes, maybe, or hours. Maybe until he went soft, uselessly, pitifully. She's shocked by the revelation of her own power, shocked by the way his body writhes, a wave of sensation—fear or desire or something else, something new—working its way through him.

"No," Brandon says, "please, don't—"

"I won't," she says soothingly. "Don't worry, I'm not going to leave you." He looks relieved. "But I could," she says, because she can't help herself. "I could if I wanted to."

"Next time," Brandon says, panting and writhing on the bed. "We'll do whatever the fuck you want, just please let me come." *Next time.* She likes the sound of that. He opens his eyes and looks at her (she loves those eyes) and says, "Please, Ma'am."

She scrambles onto the bed, straddles his hips and reaches down to slide his cock inside of her. It's never felt this good. He bucks helplessly under her weight, but he's got no leverage on the bed. She sits and takes her time and rocks in gentle circles until he stops trying to move. When he finally gives up, she leans forward and scrapes her fingernails down his chest. His body convulses, arching off the bed hard enough that she's raised off the mattress, riding him, laughing and wishing she had a lasso in the moment before she repeats her earlier action.

It hurts him. His skin is tender, and the pain from the crop is fresh, and her fingernails—her fingernails are sharp, and she is not feeling gentle. "Tell me this is okay," she says, because he looks like he's in pain and it's turning her on more than she ever dreamed it could but she loves him more than she wants to fuck him. She stops with her fingernails poised below his collarbones, ready to plan a new path down the uneven planes of his heaving chest, ready to stop.

"It's okay," he says. In the breath before she starts to hurt him again, he says, "You're okay." She gasps and digs her fingernails in deeper than she meant to and knows she's close to coming. The steady beat of his pelvis against her swollen clit, the shocks running from her nipples to her core and the ache that opened inside of her the first time she swung the crop all swell inside of her until muscles she didn't know she had are screaming. Clenching. Coming.

She scrapes her fingernails down his chest until he cries out, and then, when he inhales in a giant gasp, she tells him to come. Her voice doesn't sound like it belongs to her. (She thinks she likes the Amazon whose voice she's found. She thinks Brandon might like her, too.)

She tells him to come for her, she calls him good boy and his brilliant eyes close and his mouth falls open and she thinks, greedy and grateful and proud: *mine.*

TICKLE DAY

Jeremy Edwards

Her fantasy had been revealed weeks ago, in a spontaneous pillow-talk conference. Finally, this morning over breakfast, Steve had declared this to be Cynthia's Tickle Day.

Steve had not been a hard sell on the concept. Conveniently, he liked to bestow tickles, while Cynthia liked to receive them. To be tickled.

Just hearing that phrase in her head now—*be tickled*—made Cynthia's pussy tingle as she poured more water into the coffee machine. She could already feel hypothetical fingers rousing her pleasure points—she could close her eyes and see, stretching to the horizon, the prearranged, randomly spaced instants of teasing delight that would punctuate her day, each tickle a surprise that, under the circumstances, was really no surprise. But the magic of tickling was that it always *felt* like a surprise.

By nightfall, when Tickle Day was set to conclude in bedroom festivities, she knew her neural network would be a railway system of arousal, bustling everywhere with anticipation and need.

She refilled her coffee cup. She wanted her senses to be extra acute, and caffeine would sharpen her receptivity to every delectable moment. She—

"*Eeee!*"

There it was: the inaugural tickle. Steve had snuck up behind her while she was occupied with the coffeemaker. His forefinger had casually streaked a second and a half of magic under her pajama top, right under her rib cage.

She wiggled her ass against the front of his briefs while the echoes of the tickle rippled through her body. Her sex had gone instantly hot.

Steve slapped her butt, letting his hand linger for a quick squeeze, and then disappeared upstairs.

Cynthia's ass ground little circles into the seat of her chair while she sipped the coffee. Her cunt muscles clenched rhythmically while she tried to focus on the budget she was drafting for her newest client. Staring at the legal pad, she had to admit at least half her brain was currently devoted to listening for Steve's return.

He bounced down the stairs a few minutes later with his gym things. Cynthia cheerfully braced herself when he stopped in the kitchen to kiss her good bye. She set her pencil on the table as he approached; she was on full tickle alert. Like audience members hoping to get called onstage during a game show, each of her skin cells sizzled with the thrill of being in a place where Steve's tickle finger *might* land next.

He smiled as he leaned down to kiss her and, to her surprise, he simply kissed her. There she sat—keyed up, horny and, for the moment, absolutely untickled. She shifted tensely in her chair.

As Steve moved out of her orbit, his elbow happened to

nudge her to-do-list pencil, and it rolled off the table. "Sorry," he said, when they heard it hit the floor. He ducked out of sight to retrieve it for her.

Suddenly the hidden flesh between the last two toes of Cynthia's right foot was on fire with pleasure.

"Whoooo!" she shrieked, as she involuntarily retracted her foot from the feather her husband had evidently concealed in the cuff of his sweatshirt. Steve's skills as an amateur magician came in very handy sometimes.

And then, like lightning, it was the other foot being feather-tickled, this time on the heel. She pulled this foot away as well—a tiny bit of foot tickling was all she could handle—and her hand instinctively went to her crotch, where her pajama shorts were quietly moistening.

"See you in an hour," said Steve, with a mischievous laugh. He blew her a kiss and left for his workout.

In the shower, the normally merely invigorating pressure points of hot water felt like tickle fingers themselves, heightening and exploiting her sensitivity all over. She wriggled sensuously as the water massaged her breasts, and she actually giggled when the downpour titillated its way along her lower back and gently groped her buttocks. Her laughter reverberated across the tiles. It was as if Steve had persuaded the shower to pitch in and help him with his tickle task, to keep Cynthia deliciously primed for him while he had to be out of the house.

Wearing her towel like a micromini as she dripped onto the bath mat, Cynthia was tempted to take advantage of her pussy's stark availability to take the edge off her arousal. *For Pete's sake*, she thought to herself, *it's only nine o'clock in the morning.* How in the world was she going to get through Tickle Day without collapsing into an endless series of raunchy self-pleasuring poses—fingers wedged into her cunt while she came all over herself...vibrator shoved up inside her...nipples twisted by her own frantic fingertips...?

The answer came to her immediately: she wasn't. Her knees were bent and her towel "skirt" gaped wide over the mat. In another instant she was furiously masturbating her clit with her copious lubrication, while fantasizing that the delicate touch all over her breasts, which she'd let spill out of the towel, was a lover's feather rather than her own hand.

She came fast, with a little yelp. Then she staggered back to the bedroom, where she sank onto the bed, her thighs opening and closing in that no-man's-land between satisfaction and resurgent horniness.

Yes, she was horny, but as her breathing quieted, she recognized that she was slipping into a nap. Savoring the coolness of the pillowcase against her wet hair, she let herself drift off.

In the dream that ensued, she was eating cotton candy. She couldn't taste it, though, and the stick was incredibly slippery— so slick that she lost her grip on it, and the cotton candy landed between her legs. She tried to bend down and—

Oh! Oh-ho-ho-ho! Someone had snapped up the cotton candy before she could get to it, and he was using it to tickle her pussy. Oh, it was so good. She writhed in delight for a few moments, before waking up with her head rolling side to side on her pillow in ecstatic laughter.

There was no cotton candy, of course. But there was Steve, just withdrawing his hand from the juncture of her splayed legs. He held a silk handkerchief aloft—this was what the magician had been using to tickle her cunt lips in her sleep, under the towel. Cynthia became very aware of the damp spot beneath her on the mattress.

"I'll be in my study if you need anything," said Steve, as he left the bedroom.

Nursing a clit so rigid that she felt twinges of electricity with every motion, Cynthia now went about getting dressed. She chose her garments carefully: a sleeveless lemon top that left not only her underarms but also her midriff available, paired with a short skirt that kept the hollows behind her knee joints visible, and was loose enough to facilitate up-skirt tickling. Her feet would remain bare, the pink-polished toenails grinning up like ten tickle magnets.

She didn't waste much time deliberating over panties. She predicted she'd be changing underwear frequently today, so she'd have any number of opportunities to send in pair after favorite pair of fresh knickers, as each prior pair succumbed to her excitement. She simply lined up several pairs of bikini briefs, in an assortment of fruity stripes and solids, on the top of the dresser. Then, selecting from this display at random, Cynthia donned a pair in a color Steve had once described as "ass-kissing kiwi." Ass kissing made her think of ass tickling, of course. Consequently, she nearly felt the need to change *out* of the juicy kiwi panties before she'd even finished applying her makeup.

As for the pajama shorts she'd discarded in order to shower, these were now a fragrant flower of feminine libido on the bathroom floor. She decided to leave them there, to commemorate the tickle breakfast that had kicked things off.

The day trickled onward. Just being around Steve under the tickle mandate made Cynthia feel as if her panties—any panties—were lined with dozens of feathers, each one intent on giving her some ass tickling whenever she walked from room to room. Steve himself would hover during breaks from his office tasks, playing it cool while Cynthia got herself worked up wondering where he'd strike next. Then he'd suddenly shoot a hand up her skirt or down her leg or into her blouse out of nowhere, making her scream with wound-up horny enthusiasm, shudder as the tickles shivered through her and eventually visit the bedroom to change her underwear yet again.

When she sat at the table with a magazine after lunch, Steve faked a page turn on his own magazine and tickled her with astounding precision in the crook of her elbow. When she was on the phone with a business matter later on, he dropped by her office and massaged her shoulders for a few minutes, waiting until she was almost totally relaxed to whip out his feather. Before Cynthia knew what was happening, Steve was using it to dust the sensitive skin at the base of her neck—left side *and* right, each for two impossibly blissful seconds—after which he left her alone to explain to her client why her last remark, "I can try to have that ready," had come out sounding more like "I can try to heh-ooooh!-hch hee heheheheh-*Steee-hee-heeve!*"

By three o'clock, she was considering abandoning her efforts at productivity altogether. How could she accomplish her work, when all she could think about was where her next tickle was coming from—or rather, *when* it was coming, and on what part of her ever-ticklish anatomy it would occur?

She was managing to distract herself with some filing when Steve peeked into her office again.

"Gotta run to that meeting—back in a while."

He was gone as quickly as he'd appeared. Feeling absurdly deprived of a parting tickle, Cynthia automatically followed his trail, hurrying to her office door to see if he'd actually left the house yet.

"*Eeee!*"

No, Steve had not left the house. As a matter of fact, he had been hiding just out of her line of sight, crouching beyond her office doorway in the hall. As she'd sailed through to catch him on his way to the garage, he'd grabbed her around the waist and tickle-kissed her exposed tummy while she danced in his grasp.

"Okay," he grinned, "now I really *do* have to go. Don't forget what day it is, though." He snatched up his keys and headed out.

Cynthia stood there pleasantly flustered and intensely aroused, her knees bumping together in want while she caught her breath against the doorjamb.

Again she tried to work. With Steve out of the house and the tickle program thus on hiatus, she ought to be able to settle down and concentrate, she reasoned.

But she found that in his absence, her mind was more tickle conscious than ever. Her thoughts went to feathery fingers on naked breasts, to agile hands sprinkling themselves over a smooth belly like warm raindrops. She imagined being played like a ticklish piano—a note here, an arpeggio there—while she arched across a lover's lap. She couldn't wait to open herself up to Steve in earnest, to offer her flesh to his fingers and his feathers, to giggle and dance beneath him on the bed, a canvas to be softly painted with tickles from head to toe, entirely in small, manageable doses. She longed to feel her underpants getting pulled down by his fists, to part her legs and let his tickles kiss her there, until she was so powerfully turned on she'd settle for nothing less than his cock up her pussy and his mouth on her nipples.

So she gave up on the idea of working. After all, she reminded herself, it was she who had formally requested that

Steve put Tickle Day on the calendar—and surely she shouldn't be treating this custom-made holiday as an ordinary workday.

Now liberated from any internal pressure to be productive, and with Steve's absence dragging unaccountably on, Cynthia became so tickle obsessed that she was visited by the ghosts of tickles past, reminiscing about the first night Steve had cautiously garnished their foreplay with titillation. She remembered straddling him ravenously in her heat soon afterward, flushed and laughing from the intimate stimulation.

Would this stupid meeting of Steve's ever end? At the two-hour mark, she couldn't sit still. Her body had long been ready for the next tickle, and she was growing hungrier for it by the minute. Her latest pair of panties was so damp with her arousal, she felt like she was sitting in a puddle. It was no longer a matter of relieving the tension with a quick self-diddling; she didn't want to be diddled—she wanted to be *tickled*. Tickled and tickled and fucked.

Too bad I can't tickle myself, she reflected. It was an irrelevant thought anyway, she realized: she craved *his* fingers on her skin and *his* touch jolting little bubbles of laughter along her nerves.

But, damn, she had to do something.

As she wandered into the bedroom in her restlessness, her eyes drifted to the window. Acting on a hunch, she opened it to let in the mild evening breeze. Then she slipped off her skirt and panties, and stripped the bed of its blankets and top sheet. She lay facedown on the mattress in only her sleeveless top, with her head resting on crossed arms.

She concentrated hard to detect the gentle movement of air across the room and across her bare skin. And as the cool air breezed past her thighs and buttocks, she imagined the currents were being directed, from a distance, by Steve. She challenged herself, without moving, to let the air currents tickle up and down the crack of her ass, to give her a taste of what Steve would be doing in person when at last he returned.

The exercise was such a success that Cynthia could not, in fact, remain motionless. With her attention focused on the subtle manner in which the empty room was tickling her behind, she soon found herself gyrating—working her bottom around as if to attract the air currents, like an animal might attract its mate. Before long she had her ass high in the air, and she was quivering passionately with the microscopic tickles of countless air molecules.

She was in this position when Steve walked in on her.

"*What* are you doing?" he exclaimed kindly, smiling at her from the bedroom doorway.

She froze in place, her derriere raised to the room. "Oh, Steve, *finally*. Get over here, fast. Please!"

"I'm sorry the meeting went so long," he said as he hastened to the bed.

"It's all right, it's all right...just fucking tickle me now. Tickle me-*eee-hee-hee!*"

Her demand disintegrated into gleeful titters as his dexterous hand made its presence known all over her ass, showing the air currents how it was done. Cynthia felt all the tension breaking apart into release as her tickle-hungry flesh was soundly gratified by her husband's busy fingers. She was rocking the bed with her vigorous response, and her knees dug into the mattress. Her heels kicked at the emptiness behind her as his fingers moved from the crack to the cheeks and back, truly doing justice to her eager rear landscape until it seemed no skin cell had been left untickled.

When it was enough—when her lucky little bottom had taken every atom it could stand of tickle pleasure from Steve's fingertips—she broke away, flipping over on her back to open her legs for him. She couldn't remember when she'd ever been so turned on. As he freed his cock to enter her, her ass was still vibrating.

But Tickle Day was not over. Just as Steve's velvety shaft began tickling its way into her cunt, centimeter by centimeter, her sensors shrieked from the touch of a finger to her underarm. The armpit tickling was precisely synchronized with the penetration, and Cynthia was in heaven.

Being tickled while being fucked: could anything possibly feel better? she asked herself as she luxuriated. And Steve had chosen well. He obviously knew that his wife's underarms were a locus where she could last a little longer than some other places. Here, Steve could tickle steadily away at the same spot for as much as ten seconds at a time, and Cynthia would writhe contentedly while the stuttering waves of tickly sensation bounced through her. She clutched his idle wrist and thrust the open expanse of her tender underarm toward his tickle hand, urging him on. She was vanilla ice cream, and he was a million soft, tiny spoons.

His solid thrusts into her cunt were the perfect accompaniment to the riveting tickle strokes down the creamy hollow of her armpit—or vice versa. She was completely under the control of erogenous stimulation, and all she could do was wiggle her ass and drench Steve's cock with pussy juice, chuckling with abandon. The laughter thrum in her stomach muscles blended with the contractions of her cunt and the pulsation of her clit. She was melting into a tickled ecstasy, all giggles and shimmies and wetness.

Finally, saturated with pleasure, she closed her armpit off, reached for her clit and came in a hot flood of satisfaction. She was still laughing as she pumped Steve's cock with her twitching cunt and her toes curled around imaginary tickle feathers. Steve was coming, too; in every spasm, she could feel how worked up he'd been by the many-tickled agenda he'd been assigned this day.

On an impulse, she reached under to tickle Steve's perineum as he finished his orgasm. Her touch was accurate and skillful.

But though it didn't really make sense, it was Cynthia who squirmed and tittered when her finger played along Steve's intimate territory. One way or another, it seemed every tickle in the house was destined to be *her* property.

Especially on Tickle Day.

RELIEF

Katya Harris

I want to fuck."

"Jesus, Lila, keep your voice down."

Nicole's face was so shocked at her out-of-the-blue statement, Lila couldn't help but laugh. "Come on, Nic, no one's paying any attention to me." Actually the guys looking at her over Nicole's shoulder were looking at her plenty. Lila grinned and gave them a wink. They chuckled and turned away.

Turning her attention back to her friend, Lila said, "I just want to have some fun."

Rolling her eyes, Nicole said, "Well you don't have to scream about it."

"I certainly hope that I will though," Lila teased.

Nicole humphed, but there was a twinkle in her eye. She wasn't as bold as Lila, but they both knew that she wouldn't be going home alone tonight either.

Both of them worked at the same advertising firm and after nearly a month of killer deadlines and never-ending overtime, they both desperately needed to release the pressure that had been building inside of them. It had been Nicole's idea for them to go dancing with Dee, Andi and Mike, their other work friends. Lila hadn't even had to think about it before agreeing wholeheartedly. This was just what she needed. Drinking, dancing, flirting and then to cap the night off, a hard cock tunneling into her pussy.

"What are you guys talking about?"

"I think Lila's being naughty again."

Looking at Andi and Dee, Lila stuck out her tongue and retorted cockily, "Hey, I'm always naughty."

Dee's eyes gleamed. "True."

Arms slid around Lila's waist from behind, hugging her to a body that had been starring in her wet dreams since they'd started working together.

"Are they ganging up on you again?"

Turning her head, Lila pouted playfully at Mike. "They're being mean."

Letting her go, Mike moved to her side. Lila swallowed her disappointment and grinned at him when he told her, "Stay with me. I'll take care of you."

She wished he would. Nicole had told her before that Mike was interested in her, but Lila wasn't convinced. Sure, they flirted, but he seemed reluctant about making a move on her. It was like he was waiting for something. Lila had no idea what. They were both single, and short of scrawling I'D LIKE YOU TO FUCK ME on her forehead, she didn't know how much clearer she could be that she wanted him.

The line moved forward and they shifted with it. The closer they got to the door, the more Lila couldn't wait to get in. She chatted with her friends, but her mind was on the music she could hear throbbing on the edges of her senses. More felt than

Katya Harris

heard, it strummed the filaments of her nerves. Her body itched with the need to move, to dance. By the time the bouncers waved them through the doors of the club, Lila felt like she was about to crawl out of her skin.

Stepping in through the club's entrance was like traveling into another world. Somewhere grungier, dirtier, more raw. Designed to look like a rundown industrial building, Deliria catered to those who wanted to slum it without the actual slum. It reminded Lila of the raves she had gone to as a teenager. Even the music was more or less the same, a heavy pounding rhythm that battered its way into her body and promised to leave her ears ringing for days.

Following the others to the bar, Lila felt a wave of adrenaline rush through her. It felt like she was glowing, shining like the colored lights that strobed the darkness. She didn't want a drink.

Grabbing hold of Nicole's arm, Lila pointed first at herself and then at the packed dance floor. Nicole frowned, but nodded in understanding. Just in front of Nicole, Mike turned and raised an eyebrow in question. Lila blew him a kiss, and then she was diving through the crowd. She'd find her friends later or they'd find her. First she needed to get rid of some of this pent-up energy before she spontaneously combusted.

Bodies buffeted her as she wove her way to the middle of the dance floor. Raising her arms above her head, Lila squeezed and shimmied through the roiling mass of dancers. Limbs brushed her as she moved forward, hands reaching out to stroke over her. One grabbed her ass, squeezing hard before she twisted away.

By the time she got to the center of the writhing throng, her sweat-glazed skin hummed with sensitivity. Her heart thundered in time with the music, her blood burning like ribbons of fire threaded through her body. She felt alive, so alive. With a delirious grin, Lila gave herself over to the seduction of the music, closed her eyes and moved.

One tune finished then flowed seamlessly into another. Lila whirled and writhed, swayed and undulated. She moved as if she were fucking the air and loving every minute of it.

Strong hands slid over the curves of Lila's hip bones, pulling her back into a masculine body. She knew it was a man not just by the size of the hands, but also the rigidly hard erection pressing against her buttocks. Lila's breath caught, but she didn't stop dancing. A lazy smile flirted on her lips as she covered his hands with her own and ground her ass back into the cradle of his hips.

Wetness spilled from Lila's cunt. Dancing always aroused her, but the feel of his body moving against hers unleashed a slick torrent between her thighs. Her body, already primed by the sensuality in the atmosphere, started to throb. The thin fabric of her thong was barely a shield to the plumped up pearl of her clit. She could feel it peeking out from the lips of her pussy. Every time she moved her thighs or her dress brushed against it, a lick of heat darted through her.

He pressed in close, plastering his front to her back. Sweat stuck them together. Lila's eyes fluttered, hips swiveling to rub against him teasingly.

His hands tightened, fingertips digging into the soft expanse of her belly. Not much taller than Lila, he only had to dip his head slightly to press kisses along her shoulder. Seduced by the firmness of his lips and the rasp of his stubble on the sensitive skin of her neck, she tilted her head and let him have his way. Sliding one hand up his arm, Lila reached behind her and threaded her fingers through the soft hair at his nape. Sharp teeth nipped at her earlobe, making her jump. A hot wet tongue laved at the small pain, making her shiver. Lila's nipples hardened.

This was bad, so very naughty.

Lila loved it.

Excitement sparkled through her veins as if her blood were champagne.

His hands slid lower. The flirty hem of her ultra-short dress barely hit midthigh, so his hands didn't have to travel too far to touch skin. The tips of his fingers brushed just beneath the edge of her skirt. Lila bit her lip to keep from moaning even though no one would have heard her. Her hand, curled around his forearm, tightened. Lila could feel the hardness of his muscles beneath her fingers. She wanted to turn around, to look into his face as he touched her, but the act of not looking was so hot she didn't. Instead, she just reveled in the feel of him pressed up against her, with the planes of his chest and stomach firm against her back, the steel-hard bulge of his cock rubbing against her ass.

Fingers stroked her upper thighs. A silent question. Lila's breath hitched. Her cheeks, already red with heat and exertion, blazed even hotter.

Was she really going to do this?

Even as her mind contemplated the question, her body was acting, her legs parting. Any objections she might have had were obliterated by the brush of fingers against the sodden fabric of her thong.

All around them people were dancing, jumping, cheering. Their proximity was another turn-on, the thrill of being seen electrifying her nerves and making Lila reckless.

The air hissed from Lila's lungs. The thrum of the music

faded away, replaced by the thudding beat of her heart, the rush of blood in her ears. The crowd danced less, the movements of their bodies following a different beat. Her legs widened a little more. Her spine arched in a sharp curve, pushing her ass into him. His cock nestled in between her buttocks. On her shoulder, his lips moved. A smile.

Impatient fingers nudged her thong aside. Lila gasped and then groaned, the noise swallowed by the music. Her clit throbbed demandingly, her cunt spilling creamy arousal over his fingers as he slid them through the saturated folds of her sex. He didn't tease her and she was glad. She didn't want to be teased.

Lila's mouth gaped. Two thick fingers speared her, plunging deep into the hot wetness of her pussy. A pinch of pain brightened her pleasure as his touch forced her to open, stretching the delicate muscles ruthlessly.

Rapture streaked up Lila's spine, forked like lightning over the inside of her skull.

His other hand coasted up her body, grazed her pebbled nipple and wrapped around her throat. Tilting her head back, he tormented the tender skin of her neck with lips and teeth and tongue. He pumped his fingers into her, the heel of his palm grinding against her swollen clit. Her hips moved, helping him work her. Each stroke pushed her closer and closer to orgasm until, with a shattered cry, she broke. Her body strained, every muscle rigid with the onslaught of pleasure. She didn't know if the lights dancing before her eyes were in her head or the club's light show.

Lila's body clung greedily to his fingers as he slid them free of her. From the corner of her half-hooded eyes she watched him bring his hand up to his mouth. She whimpered at the thought of him sucking away the slick juices of her orgasm. Her belly tightened in renewed arousal. Pressing her hips back, she rubbed against his erection in blatant invitation.

She felt movement behind her. Lila had only a few seconds to wonder what he was doing and then his fingers were yanking her thong to the side, the blunt head of his dick sliding through the folds of her pussy. She sucked in a breath, her mouth falling open. Her thoughts scrambled as he overshot, the ridge of his cock catching her oversensitive clit. A jolt of sensation rocketed through her and then his dick, hard and thick, was pushing into her.

She'd thought they'd go somewhere else. The toilets. A dark corner, which Deliria had plenty of. Outside maybe. Lila hadn't thought that he'd fuck her in the middle of a crowd of people, but she found he felt too good for her to care.

Trembling, her hand tightening in his hair, Lila arched her hips backward and let him in. Fabric rubbed against her ass; she realized her dress still covered her, and he'd only unzipped himself enough to get his cock out. The thought gave her an inexplicable thrill. Pushing back, she took every inch of his cock into her pussy. He was big, deliciously so, but she was so very wet from arousal and orgasm that he slid into her in one smooth, powerful glide.

For a moment, disbelief stilled the world. She was letting someone fuck her on the dance floor. Was she insane? Then he started to move against her, in her. Strong thrusts as his hands gripped her hips with bruising strength. In and out, his cock so big she could feel its thick veins rubbing inside of her and driving her crazy with lust.

Sensations bombarded her. The music, the other dancers, the dizzying lights, his breath hot on her neck and his hard dick moving in her spasming pussy. Lila's senses reeled. She couldn't control the pleasure spinning through her, couldn't stop it. Her cunt squeezed his shuttling cock tighter and tighter, the friction a delicious pressure that suddenly exploded in an incandescent starburst. A scream tore from her throat and was quickly rendered silent by the blaring music.

Pleasure cascaded through her. Diamond-tipped needles raked over her senses, scoring deeper when she felt the thick length of him pulse deep inside her. His fingers bit into her hips; vibrations rumbled against her spine as he groaned. Heat blossomed in her belly, softening the last jagged peaks of her orgasm.

They stood, joined together and motionless in the seething mass of dancers, both breathing hard. Then he slipped his cock out of her. Lila whimpered. Fingers tugged her underwear back into place. Hot wetness leaked out of her pussy. A little escaped her thong and trickled down her thigh. She brought her legs together, smearing the sticky trail.

Lila could feel him moving behind her, zipping himself up.

Hands on her shoulders spun her around. Mike grinned at her, eyes gleaming playfully in the flashing lights. Lila had a moment to feel not shocked, and then he was kissing her. His firm lips caught at hers, his tongue flicking out to lick across her mouth. Lila's eyelids fluttered; her breath hitched. She leaned forward for more, but he was already melting into the crowd with a wink and a smirk.

Lila stared after him. Her pussy was sore, sticky with his come. Part of her wanted to go after him and drag him home for some more, but she figured she'd find him later.

A smile pulling at her lips, Lila let the music take her over again.

JAILBAIT TORCH SONG

Valerie Alexander

Lyla tried to be a good single mother. She'd finished her degree despite getting pregnant at nineteen, had gotten a good job as a network engineer, and bought a house in the most affluent neighborhood in her small town. All of this was to provide her ten-year-old son, Jax, with the kind of life people predicted he wouldn't have without a father. The right friends from the right families, connections, memories, the whole Norman Rockwell dream. Usually she succeeded and usually it came at a cost she didn't like paying: specifically, a lack of available men. All of the local men seemed to be someone's husband. On a few occasions she'd found herself eyeing a beautiful young man only to realize, mortified, that she'd been lusting for someone's older teenage son.

Part of being a good single mother was cooking good meals, which is why she was laboring over an elaborate marinara sauce when the doorbell rang one January evening.

She opened the door to find a tall, lanky boy on her stoop. He had hair that fell between brown and blond, blue-green eyes and honeyed skin so flawless she felt a physical pang of envy. They looked at each other without speaking for three beats too long.

"Hi," he said finally.

She decided that he had the wrong house. He looked a little old to be in high school, but no one hung around this town after graduation. He was probably here to pick up a friend who lived in the neighborhood.

She pushed a loose strand of auburn hair back into her ponytail. "Who are you looking for?"

"Uh, you. I mean, anyone." He fumbled with a clipboard. "I'm a senior on the basketball team, and we're trying to raise money for camp by selling magazines."

He was here to sell something. Of course. About twice a month some high-school group rang her bell, trying to finance new uniforms or a class trip. She kept her gaze trained on his clipboard while he showed her the selections so her eyes wouldn't betray this baffling sensation of her heart skittering around in her chest.

"Sure," she said. "That *Young Explorers* magazine, I'll get that for my son."

"You're married?" He sounded shocked.

"No," she said.

She kept her eyes away from him as he followed her into the kitchen, tracking snow on the tile. Maintaining a rigidly cool smile—*no, she wasn't flustered at all, there were no butterflies in her stomach*—she wrote him a check. His name was Tanner. He sat on a stool at the breakfast bar and commented on how good the sauce smelled, his eyes locked on her face.

She handed him the check and smiled tightly. "Thanks for coming by."

"You're welcome." He hesitated. "Well, I guess that's it."

"The sauce is going to burn," she said. "I don't mean to be rude but..."

"Sorry." He hustled to the door, shoulder brushing the door-jamb—he wasn't quite at home in that towering body yet—and stopped again to look back at her. She looked at his blue jacket, which was what the high-school athletes wore around town, and then at the dark-green Jeep Cherokee parked outside. Then she met his eyes. He was watching her with blazing, naked hope.

Her stomach plunged to her feet and she stepped away. "Thanks," she said again and then, "Good luck with your season."

"You should come to a game," he said.

"Maybe. Good night."

Lyla shut the door. She couldn't get back in the kitchen fast enough, back to the domestic innocence of the marinara on the stove and Jax's karate class schedule on the refrigerator. *That didn't really just happen*, she told herself. She hadn't really just swooned over a high-school kid. She looked at the melting sludge tracked in from his sneakers and reached for a paper towel. Then she let it melt on its own, leaving a faint dirty mark on the tile that her eyes returned to repeatedly over the next few days.

A week later she found herself sitting at the train station, watching the parking lot across the street. Afternoon was turning to evening and a heavy snow was coming down; she had dropped Jax off at karate class and now she couldn't stop looking at a dark-green Jeep Cherokee coated with frothy snow outside the bagel shop.

He could be eighteen, she said to herself. And then: *but this is still crazy.*

When she went in, a thin, sullen-looking boy watched her from the counter. Her heart fell with a mix of disappointment and relief.

"Can I help you?"

"Yes—a sesame bagel. Regular cream cheese." She dug into her purse.

To the right of her vision, a door swung open. "Hey," Tanner said. "Lyla."

She turned. "Oh! Hi!" Her voice sounded false. "So this is where you work."

"Yeah, just at night." His eyes were as alive and enamored as an animal's. "I'm eighteen, so I can close."

I'm eighteen. Message delivered. She took out a five-dollar bill to pay the cashier. "So how have you been?"

"All right. I didn't think I'd see you again."

"Well—" She accepted the change back. "It's a small town."

His eyes were rapidly studying her coat, her hair. Eighteen—or so he said—and intent on escalating a bad idea. His long body gave the impression of straining toward her like a dog on a leash. "So did your magazine come yet?"

"No. Didn't you say it would take a month?" She took the bagged bagel from the cashier. "See you later."

He backed away with a contrived boyish smile and a wave. Outside the sky was a heavy gray and visibility was poor through the thick flurry of flakes. After starting the car, she sat in the driver's seat. She gazed through the windshield, her heart hammering wildly. Suddenly there was a knock on the window. She lowered it and a soft wall of snow sprinkled onto her jeans.

He leaned into the car. "I just wanted to tell you that we have a home game tomorrow night. You should come."

"Yeah, I can't do that."

"Why not?"

"Because I don't have a reason to be there," she said. "Because it would look weird."

He walked away. Puzzled, she waited for him to return and say good-bye. Then the passenger door swung open and he climbed in the car.

Oh no. Quickly she elevated her window. "I have to pick up my son," she said.

Then his hand was in her hair, hauling her across the seat and onto his long body as if she were weightless. He was shaking. His arms went around her, pulling her against his chest so hard she could feel his heart thumping. He kissed her with almost feverish desperation, his cold hands sliding up under her sweater and under her bra. "Don't stop me," he muttered into her mouth and then she was grinding all over the promise of his hard cock, humping him with abandon.

In a flash, he had the seat down and was pulling her over him. She pushed his shirt up, burying her face in his warm skin. Then a car door slammed nearby.

Lyla sat up in alarm. "Don't stop," Tanner urged, trying to pull her back down, but she was already adjusting her sweater and climbing back into her seat.

"You have to go," she said in a shaky voice.

He didn't protest. Instead he kissed her good-bye—that earlier plea in his eyes was now replaced with a self-satisfied smile, she noticed—and climbed out of the car.

Eighteen. In high school. It was worse than crazy, it was wrong. And yet his silky hair, that hard, athlete's body—she bit her pillow as she fingered herself that night, wishing it was him.

Lyla's closest friend in the neighborhood was Anne from the cul de sac behind hers. At forty-two, Anne was a little older than she was. Her kids were already in college so Lila was surprised when she called the next evening and invited her to the basketball game. "My niece cheers for the varsity team. I know it's not exactly exciting but we could go out to eat after."

Lyla took a deep breath. "Sure, that'd be fun."

She hadn't been in a high school gymnasium in over a decade. But as soon as they passed through the double doors, her senses were flooded with nostalgia: the echo of a rebounding ball, the glare of the ceiling lights, the pounding sneakers and the harsh buzzer of the scoreboard—it all came back to her. She didn't look at the court as Anne led her up to the third row of the bleachers.

A ref's whistle pierced the gym. Lyla permitted herself a glance at the floor as five lanky boys in blue and white jerseys ran down the court. Yes, there was Tanner's brownish-blond head. Her face went hot.

A buzzer blared through the gym and the players stopped. Tanner glanced at the bleachers, turned away, then pivoted and looked back at her. A triumphant grin spread over his face.

"Hold on," Anne said in a low voice. "How do you know Tanner Lichton?"

"I don't. He sold me a magazine when the team was doing some fundraising."

Anne looked at her flatly. Lyla blushed. "He's a nice kid—"

"Cut the crap," Anne said. "I saw the way he smiled at you."

She opened her mouth to lie, but couldn't. As Anne waited, she finally managed, "Look, he *is* eighteen."

"Holy shit." Anne whistled under her breath. She looked out at the court, where the players launched back into scrambling, shooting, running chaos. "Well, be careful. But I can't say I blame you."

Her son was off at a friend's for the night. She paced the living room, her nerves thrumming like live wires. She'd left the basketball game without speaking to Tanner, despite the beseeching looks he'd sent her from the court. *Of course I'm not going to sleep with him,* she'd said to Anne and she half-meant it at the time, but now that she was cleaning the kitchen, she couldn't deny that her body felt flushed and electric, anticipating—something.

It came in a knock on the back patio doors.

Her heart leapt with ridiculous happiness. She opened the door to find him towering over her in his blue varsity jacket. At least he'd known not to come to the front door where her neighbors would see. But then she panicked.

"My son's not here but if for some reason he came home—" she began.

He leaned down to kiss her. "No one's going to find out."

Still nervous, she took him down in the basement where bags of wrapping paper and Jax's discarded video games were piled on the carpet. He pushed her onto the sofa.

I'm not really about to sleep with a high-school kid, she thought, but Tanner was groping her breasts and kissing her with that same wolfish hunger as yesterday, as if she were a city he wanted to plunder. He stripped her naked in seconds and then he was unzipping his pants and rubbing his hard dick on her stomach. This wasn't going to go like her few trysts had over the last few years, methodical sex that meant nothing but skin and sweat. This was going to count in some new and visceral way, and that loss of control scared her as he fell back on the sofa cushions, naked and hard from his thighs to his chest.

He pulled her down on top of him until she could feel him trembling. "Please don't stop," he said, and kissed her again.

Lyla pushed him back, wanting to regain control before he overwhelmed her completely. But with a grunt of frustration, he pulled her hips onto his face. She balanced herself on the sofa as his tongue washed over her cunt, rocking back and forth on what felt like a snake undulating inside her. Her nipples ached in the basement chill as she rode his face, humping his mouth without shame. Tanner drew the swollen seed of her clit into his mouth and sucked it, working his fingers inside her. His balls were so tight she knew he was going to come at any moment.

"Condom," she said, panting.

Tanner's face was the same burning scarlet as his cock. He half-lunged off the sofa, retrieving a condom from his discarded jeans, and quickly peeled it down over his swollen shaft. She sat back on him, slowly engulfing his dick. He was big enough to stretch her, and she sighed with faint soreness and pleasure as she at last settled on the base of his cock.

Tanner was biting his lip with the obvious effort to hold back. "Please," he said through clenched teeth. She didn't have time to ask *Please what?* before he took over, grabbing her hips and bouncing her hard and fast, driving his cock into her over and over. Lyla succumbed with a groan, letting him fuck her into a mindless, animal euphoria. She played with her clit until her face and body flooded with heat and then she came in a thudding, flooding gush. Tanner groaned and pulled her down on his chest, spasming inside her.

She listened to his heartbeat as his fingers lazily moved in her hair. *I just had sex with an eighteen-year-old,* she thought.

"I could feel you come," he said with a mix of pride and amazement.

She bit back her smile. He was rubbing her head so tenderly that she barely noticed a few minutes later when he tilted her head toward his newly stiffening cock: he was getting hard again already. She sucked him into her mouth, the salty taste of his precome lacing her tongue, but once again he took over, gripping her ass with a long groan and then dragging her behind the couch. Rough and wordless as a caveman, he bent her over the back of the couch until she was facedown with her legs dangling in the air.

This time he fucked her with more control than before, his cock driving in and out of her from behind until she was screaming into the cushions. Her legs kicked helplessly as his fingers worked her clit until she howled out her orgasm, her pussy clenching again and again.

This time she was the one who couldn't stop shaking as he held her on the sofa. "It's cold," she said self-consciously.

"I'll keep you warm," he said. He seemed massive as he covered her, an endless stretch of warm skin and muscle and silky hair. His cock still wasn't completely soft.

"You're really eighteen, right?"

"I really am. Do you want to see my driver's license?"

"Kind of."

After they got dressed, he dug out his wallet and showed her his license in the weak basement light. She looked at it, then looked up at him. He kissed her. "I can come back tomorrow night," he said.

Spring flooded in on a tide of late nights in the basement and the occasional rainy weekend afternoon in a hotel room. Basketball season had ended and Tanner had lacrosse after school now. Because she lived within walking distance of the woods behind the high school, sometimes she would meet him after practice in the equipment shed. She knew it was stupid to risk such exposure, knew the gossip would be lethal if she was caught sleeping with a high-school senior. But in the shadows of sunset, watching him peel off his sweat-damp uniform as she leaned back amongst the goal nets and lacrosse sticks, she only wanted to bury herself in his skin and hair and cock for as long as she could.

"The word on the street," Anne said in early June, "is that Shannon Mariner saw a boy going into your backyard at one a.m."

"What the hell was Shannon Mariner doing scoping out my backyard at one a.m.?"

"You knew it would happen sooner or later."

"Well, he *is* eighteen. It's not like this is illegal."

Anne looked at her.

"I know," she said. "Trust me, I've thought about it a million times."

That night she walked through the woods and crossed the starlit lacrosse field to the equipment shed. As always, her nose filled with the smells of rank cleats and grass and faintly, the smell of come; they clearly weren't the only ones who used the shed. Teammates in secret love met here or teachers maybe, students cutting out of study hall. The door swung open and

Tanner pushed her against the wall, lifting her up by the hips and kissing her. His erection prodded against her and his massive hands groped her with that voracious desperation she loved, tugging down her jeans as if her pussy was his lifeline. He flipped her onto all fours a minute later; there was a rip of a condom foil and then his cock drove into her from behind, fucking her long and hard until she rocked back and forth on the cement, her knees aching.

Afterward he cradled her in the crook of his arm, spreading his shirt under her back to buffer the chilly floor.

"My neighbor saw you," she said. "Apparently everyone is talking about how I had a kid coming over in the dead of the night."

"How is that their business?"

"It's not. But it's how life in a small town works."

"That's fucking ridiculous," he said. "I'm eighteen. I'm an adult. Not to mention I'm graduating in two weeks."

Don't be in such a hurry, is what she wanted to say but she didn't.

She never knew if Shannon Mariner had identified Tanner or the town gossip network eventually connected them—but his parents abruptly arranged for him to spend the summer working at his uncle's office across the country. There was one last night in the equipment shed, the high school now closed for the summer and the fields rhythmic with crickets around them—and then he was gone. After ten nights of emails and Skype and a hollow yearning filling her bones every night, she told him it was time for both of them to move on.

"We don't have to stay for the whole game," Anne said. "I know you're not a big football fan but my niece was nominated for Homecoming Queen."

Shades of the game where she saw Tanner. But Lyla smiled, because it was October now and she could think of Tanner without her gut clenching. "Sounds good."

The bleachers and the track around the football field were crowded under the lights. She spotted Jax and his friends, now in sixth grade, traveling from under the bleachers to the concession stand in pursuit of a group of girls. Lyla contented herself with a wave, which he discreetly returned.

Then Tanner tapped her on the shoulder.

Somehow this time it didn't matter who saw them talk. They walked down toward the red concession stand but didn't get in line, lingering on the grass until he said, "Let's go for a walk."

He went toward the woods and cut back around toward the equipment shed, while she walked across the parking lot to the lacrosse field. Tanner pulled her inside so roughly her boots left the ground. That familiar scent of come and sweat and freshly mown grass filled her nostrils and then he was pinning her against the wall, kissing her with that same demanding fever. It had been four months since she'd touched him but nothing had changed. His hands slid under her sweater, his fingers digging into her breasts before tugging down her jeans. He bit her arms, her neck, fingered her roughly, and it occurred to some distant part of her that really she should have trained him to be a slower and more artful lover—but she never had because she loved the sensation of being craved and devoured.

He rolled onto the floor, naked, and pulled her on top of him. "I've missed you," he grunted, as he worked his cock inside her. "I've missed you so fucking much." She locked her knees around him and then he was all the way inside her, ramming her in relentless, masterful ownership. A lost ache broke open inside her, flooding her with nostalgia as his arms wrapped around her, holding her ribs and breasts and hips against him.

The equipment shed was hot and airless, the thick smell of sex breathing around them. Her long hair hung in his face as she rode him, his breath on her neck as they fucked in a brutal, seamless rhythm that seemed to sear her skin. Tanner rolled her over until she was facedown on the floor, the cement thrillingly cool against her inflamed body as his cock drove into her from behind. She bit her arm, her skin wet with sweat, to keep from screaming or crying as he thrust into her again and again.

He was pawing, pulling at her ass. Muttering unintelligible things under his breath and panting as he fucked her. She gripped her hair, feeling her whole body blaze alive with light just as she ejaculated helplessly and ecstatically all over the floor.

He groaned and crushed her against his chest as he came. Then he rolled off her and held her against him without speaking for a long while.

She was almost asleep when he began talking about Thanksgiving vacation, telling her that he was going skiing with his roommate in Telluride.

"It's good that you like your roommate," she said.

"Yeah, we'll probably get a place off campus next year." He paused. "You know, I drove home this weekend—my school is only five hours away."

She got up and looked out at the moonlit lacrosse field. "You're in college now," she said. "It's time for you to..."

He watched her with a brooding face. She didn't finish. "So many girls are going to fall for you," she said instead.

His lips twisted in a cocky smile. "Who can blame them?"

He got dressed and they kissed good-bye. "Christmas break," he said, pausing at the door. "Just think about it."

"I will."

She waited for him to leave the shed first, even though the game was over and the parking lot had to be empty by now. She looked around at the lacrosse sticks and goal nets, knowing she would never see them again. Then she went out into the mellow October night and began the walk home, her heart as light as the dry leaves that scattered and blew away with the wind.

RED LIPSTICK

Erzabet Bishop

I leaned over my counter in the makeup department and sighed. It was past time. Melody Aires had been here every Thursday night for the last eight weeks and I was beginning to worry that tonight she wasn't going to show. Glancing in one of the mirrors, I dabbed at my lipstick, making sure it was perfect. Wouldn't do for it to be smudged.

My coworker was busy with a mother and daughter who seemed to be trying on every shade of pink and red lip gloss and blush combinations in the entire department. That was fine. Joanie had the patience of Job. Mine however, was running out. I looked at my watch again: 8:10. Maybe she wasn't coming after all. I began to tidy up the register area and tried to swallow my disappointment.

The faint clicking of heels on the parquet floor had my heart leaping in my chest. *She was here.* I closed my eyes to catch my breath. My black dress suddenly felt too tight and constrictive.

"Good evening, Francesca." Melody smiled, her ivory skin

a perfect contrast to her wavy black hair. Her lips were scarlet red and as usual, her makeup perfect.

"Good evening." I let the smile I was bursting to show come into my voice. "I was beginning to worry that you wouldn't be by for your usual visit."

"Would you have missed me then?" Her smile turned up slightly at the edges and a wicked glint took over her eyes.

I felt my nipples tighten and my pussy begin to moisten in desire. Her full lips beckoned, and not for the first time I wondered how it would feel if I just leaned over the counter ever so slightly and touched them to mine. I wanted to taste her inner sweetness and run my hands over that wonderfully soft flesh. Her breasts were molded against her tight black sweater, and her short leather mini left little to the imagination. Her legs went on for miles and ended in gorgeous black fuck-me shoes. Was she wearing underwear? My pulse quickened at the thought of finding out.

"Oh, yes," I purred and then remembered where I was. *God, you are such a fucking perv. Get your head out of your ass and do your job before she complains.*

"Hmmm." Her eyes met mine and held them. "Now that is interesting." Melody winked, then walked down to the lipstick samples, staring at them like she had never seen them before.

I fidgeted and tried to block out my inappropriate flirtatiousness. Smoothing my skirt, I took a deep breath, counted to ten and made my way over to her to offer my assistance.

"Did you find a new color?"

Melody smiled and held up two tubes for my inspection. All traces of our earlier awkwardness were gone. "What do you think?"

I took the lipstick and went to retrieve cotton swabs and a

box of tissues. Opening them up, I slid the stick portion down the lipstick to gather enough for her to sample. My hands trembled at the thought of her covering her lips with an offering of mine. Watching her never failed to make me wet, and since I was already pushing my own boundaries tonight, I would have to be extra careful.

The first sample was Tangled Roses. Handing her the stick, I watched as she wiped off her old color and gently applied the new one. Lips pursed, she spread the creamy reddish-pink blend and I sighed, letting my mouth fall open. Every minute movement of her fingers as they spread the color over her lips sent little shivers down my back and a jolt of awareness between my thighs.

"What do you think?" Melody pursed her lips into a moue and smiled.

"Beautiful."

"I like it. Let's see the other one, too." Melody was already wiping off the Tangled Roses and getting ready for the new sample.

"Sure." I uncapped the second tube and scraped off a line of color. Rhapsody was the name, and I couldn't agree more. It was one of my favorites.

She took the swab from my trembling fingers and smoothed the dark, blood-red lipstick over her lips. We both looked in the mirror and I nodded. It was perfect.

"I'll take them both. Give me two of the Rhapsody."

I gathered the boxes of new lipstick from the drawers and ran them through the register. Melody handed me her credit card and the sale was completed. Placing her receipt in the bag, I turned to give it to her.

"Here," she said, sliding a red envelope across the counter.

I looked at her, perplexed. "What's this?"

She met my questioning gaze with a solid one of her own. "I'm taking a chance on you, Francesca. Be there and follow the instructions to the letter." Melody opened the bag with her purchase and drew out one box of Rhapsody. "Wear it."

I started to protest, but she spun on her heel. I watched her walk away. Skirt tight on her ass, she marched down the center of the store as if she owned it. The envelope sat on the counter where she had placed it, untouched.

"What's that?" Joanie appeared out of nowhere, and I jumped.

"Nothing." I scooped up the envelope and lipstick and slid it into a pocket on my short black apron and tried to get my mind off the slickness coating my thighs and the woman who haunted my waking dreams.

> *You have been cordially invited as a guest to the Parlor for a night of bondage and discipline.*
>
> *Attendance is requested for 7:00 p.m. on November 12, 2013. Punctuality is essential.*
>
> *Attire: Black.*

I stared at the invitation in my hand and still couldn't believe it. *A bondage club? What the hell was I doing?* Written in spidery black script on red paper that probably cost more than I made in a week at the store, the invitation lay on my lap as I sat in the car. It was 6:55. I had five minutes to either make it to the door or turn around and forget this had ever happened. My hands shook as I pulled out the lipstick Ms. Aires had requested I wear. Smoothing it over my lips, I made up my mind. This was the chance to do something I had always dreamed of.

The club was on the outskirts of town and to anyone without a discerning eye, it could be just another country manse, hidden behind an iron gate and immaculately kept grounds. The line of cars waiting for the valet was long, but as I edged closer, I realized I would be able to be punctual. The valet was at my driver's side door and suddenly it was decision time.

Opening the car door, I stepped out and wobbled on my newly purchased, black, four-inch heels. My short black dress was tasteful and elegant. I had obsessed for days, looking to make just the right first impression. I had twisted my russet-colored hair into an updo and worn my best diamond earrings and necklace. Slamming the car door on my insecurities, I walked briskly to the entrance and handed the doorman my invitation.

"Good evening." He smiled and waved me inside. "To the right, please."

I stepped through the elegant door and into another universe.

"Hello." A young blonde woman in a leather collar and nothing else approached me. "What is your name?"

"Francesca." I smiled, nervous about what was going to happen next. I was trying very hard not to stare at her chest. Her nipples were pierced with rhinestone studs that flickered as she moved.

"I am Bianca. Please follow me into the next room." Her eyes twinkled with amusement as she caught me staring. I followed without another word.

"You will disrobe and place your belongings in one of these lockers."

"What?" I panicked, bile rising up in my throat. No one had said anything about wearing anything other than black.

Bianca rolled her eyes and dragged me over to a colorful

rack of corsets and costumes. "This is a fetish party, among other things. You have to change out of your street clothes and put on one of these. Some of the guests are regulars, but since this is your first time at the Parlor, you get to pick something from the collection."

"Fetish?"

"Yes. Erotic attachment to objects. Mistress Melody has shared with me your fixation on women's lips and lipstick. I myself have noticed your attention to some of my, um, attributes." Bianca blushed prettily and began to prowl through the rack in search of something. "Here." She eyed my cleavage. "I think this will fit, but you really do have to undress. Time is short and you are due out on the floor momentarily."

A flush crept up my neck as I glanced down at the object in my hand. A corset. An actual, honest to goddess corset. My inner folds clenched and I found myself growing weak in the knees. "How did you know?" I whispered.

Bianca patted my back and proceeded to unzip my dress. "Step out." I did and she nodded at my choice of thigh-high stockings and black silk panties. "Very nice. The bra has to go, too."

I unhooked it and handed it over. Bianca hung the dress and slid the bra over the top of the hanger, placing it in my locker. She took the corset from me and I marveled at the sea of hooks and loops.

"Hold up your arms."

I lifted them up and Bianca maneuvered the corset around my torso. As she worked the fastenings, a sudden jerk had me gasping for breath.

"Okay. Hold on to something. My knee is about to meet the middle of your back."

I swore as the breath was knocked out of me once again and then the grunting and finger fumbling ceased. Bianca came around the front. "Okay, now pop those boobs."

"What?"

Bianca rolled her eyes. "You have to pull your cleavage up or the corset won't sit right."

"Oh!" I laughed, feeling stupid. Plunging my hands into the cups of the corset, I lifted out my breasts and set them back in properly. The difference was immediate. I looked into the mirror and hardly recognized myself. The corset was ravishing in shades of dark red with black accents, making my eyes look black and my lips a very full red. I was beautiful.

"Much better." Bianca looked me up and down. "One more coat of lipstick and you are ready."

I went over to my purse and applied another coat, luxuriating in the feel of the lipstick on my lips.

"Time to go." Bianca held the door and I tossed the lipstick back into my purse and ran after her.

The main room was almost empty and this spurred my guide to move even faster. "Hurry!"

My heels wobbled as I struggled to run down the hall and breathe at the same time. Corset wearing was not as easy as it looked.

When we reached the main door, Bianca stopped. "Okay. Now, go in. The presentation should be almost over; then you mingle. You will find your Mistress Aires and she will claim you as her guest tonight. Good luck."

Opening the door, I walked right in on a presentation and all eyes turned my way. An enigmatic man in a tux who'd been speaking paused and looked at me with mild disdain.

"As I was saying, we need a volunteer for the next part

of this evening's presentation. How lovely that this late little submissive has turned up just in time."

I swallowed. Oh my goddess. He was talking about me.

"You there, young woman in the corset. Please come here."

My legs were shaking. I felt the weight of hundreds of eyes on me as I made my way to the stage.

"Yes, Sir."

"Good. Now, who claims this young woman as their guest?"

"I do." Melody Aires stood, a vision in black leather and platform shoes.

"What do you think we should do with a submissive who is in need of a lesson on punctuality?"

Ms. Aires walked up the steps to the stage. "I think a flogging would be in order, Sir Anthony."

"Ms. Aires?" I whimpered, scared out of my mind.

"Francesca. Come here." Ms. Aires pointed to two hoops that hung from the very top of the curtains. "I want you to hold on to these and not let go." She smacked me on the ass and walked over to a table to retrieve something.

This was not going like my fantasy at all. I had read plenty of erotic novels and knew it was supposed to be safe, sane and consensual. I hadn't given anyone here permission to do anything, had I? Bile crept up my throat again as I reached up to grab the rings. My breasts threatened to spill out of my corset and I wondered how I was going to be flogged if I was still wearing it.

I heard movement behind me and felt a tug at my laces. *Oh goddess!*

"No!" I tried to wiggle away but Ms. Aires grabbed me by the hair. A flood of moisture pooled in my pussy and I moaned.

"I knew I was right about you, little Francesca. Now, you have put me in the embarrassing and awkward situation of punishing you when we aren't even officially seeing each other. If I hadn't claimed you, some else might have. I suspect you would not have liked that, would you?"

"No, Ma'am," I whimpered.

"Good. Now I am going to flog you, very gently. To do this, I will need to remove your corset. If it is your choice, we can continue. I haven't been coming to your counter for months because I actually need thirty tubes of lipstick, mind you. This just didn't turn out exactly how I'd planned it to go. Now, if you agree, I would like you to face the back of the stage and I will unlace you. You will be flogged and then you and your pretty pussy will be mine for the evening. Is that agreeable to you?"

I stared at her in shock. "I…um…yes, Ma'am."

"That is fine. Now, turn around unless you want all these fine people to see your lovely breasts."

"Yes, Ma'am." Blushing, I turned my back to the audience and felt Mistress Aires begin to tug at my laces. After a few moments, she freed me from the corset and I was left to hang from the rings in nothing but my black silk panties and thigh-high stockings.

"Good evening, ladies and gentlemen. Please forgive the late intrusion of my new submissive, Francesca. She is quite new to the scene and this is her first party. Can we please welcome my new pet?"

The crowd clapped and tittered with laughter as I hung my head in embarrassment.

"Excellent. I have chosen to flog Francesca tonight to demonstrate the many uses of a flogger, from the lightest touch to the sharpest sting."

I felt the whoosh of the leather strips against my back on the first blow; they landed much like a feather against my skin. The second pass was not as fluid. The strips snapped along the expanse of my back, causing me to wince and cry out. Tears escaped my eyes before I even realized I was crying. I had to bite my lip to hold back the sob that threatened to escape.

"One more pass, Francesca." Mistress Aires ran the handle of the instrument against my ass and let it delve between my thighs. "You can also use the flogger to entice and excite a reaction from your submissive that will leave them in a puddle of lust. Use the handle just so to flick her clit to attention just before striking and you are guaranteed to have a slave more than happy to bend to your will."

The final pop of the flogger against the side of my ass sent my senses reeling and I groaned as moisture seeped from between my legs.

"Thank you, ladies and gentlemen, for your gracious attention. Sir Anthony, I leave the rest of the floggings to your expert hand."

She came around and pulled my shaking hands from the rings, tugging my body against hers. "Walk with me." I let her lead me, bare breasted, off the stage and out a side door.

"I have a room set aside. Come, I will have your clothing and personal items sent for." I followed Mistress Aires down a long hallway until we reached a door that she unlocked with a key card.

"Come in and sit down, please."

I shakily sat down on the massive bed. "Well, that wasn't how I envisioned our first encounter."

Mistress Aires laughed. "Nor I. Now, how about I live up to my promise and make it up to you?"

She moved between my thighs and I froze.

"Do you wish to use a safeword? We are probably a little past that formality, but if you like..."

"Marmalade."

She laughed and nodded. "Well then, marmalade it is." Her face vanished between my thighs and my panties went airborne, along with my shoes.

Her lips nibbled along my inner thighs and her fingers entered me three deep, filling me instantly. I cried out as her lips moved to my eager and throbbing clit, sending me into orbit almost immediately.

"Oh goddess!" I screamed and bucked against her face. She withdrew her fingers and pulled my pussy closer. Her tongue licked my sex from front to back before she began to fuck me with it. With her thumb working my clit, she sucked and licked my hungry cunt until I howled her name in sobbing ecstasy.

"Now, wasn't that worth a little flagellation?" She wiped her moist face on the bedsheet and pounced on me. "What do you want to do next?"

I smiled at her, suddenly shy. "Well, I kind of wanted to watch you put on that new red lipstick."

She laughed. "And then what?"

"Then I am going to find out what's under that skirt. That is, if you don't mind, Mistress." I bit my lip and lowered my eyes, trying unsuccessfully to be coy.

"Oh, I think that can be arranged." She slapped me on the ass and got up to find the tube of lipstick that had started it all.

My night was looking better and better.

SOMETHING SLEAZY

Elizabeth Coldwell

Let's do something sleazy this weekend." Brett regarded me over the lip of his coffee mug.

I continued to spread apricot conserve on my buttered toast. "What exactly did you have in mind?" I kept my tone casual, trying not to let him know how much he'd piqued my interest with those words.

The last time he'd suggested "something sleazy," we'd found ourselves checking into a down-market hotel under false names, and pretending we had respective spouses who we were cheating on. I could still recall the feel of the cheap nylon coverlet under my knees, and the way the bed's padded velour headboard had banged against the wall with every thrust as Brett fucked me from behind, his hands gripping my hips hard and his breath harsh and urgent in my ear. We'd had the kind of quick, animalistic sex we'd largely given up in favor of long, leisurely sessions on a Sunday morning. I knew acting out one of his favorite fantasies had added some much-needed spice to our marriage.

Not that things had become boring, exactly, but when you've been together as long as we have, there's always the danger that you'll sink into a comfortable routine and forget about the hot, frantic encounters that made the relationship so enjoyable in the early days.

"Oh, I don't know," he said, as if the idea had only just occurred to him. "I was thinking maybe we could take a trip to the park later on."

He gave me a moment to let the idea sink in. We didn't visit the park often; it was on the other side of the city, and when I wanted to exercise our little bichon frise, Millie, I usually took her on a short circuit that encompassed our local shops and back. She was getting too old to want to go very far, and I had a deadline that meant I couldn't spare much time out of my working day to accommodate her. It made more sense to combine her walk with my chores.

But a couple of Sundays ago, the weather had been unseasonably fine and Brett had been restless. He'd persuaded me to step away from the laptop for a while so we could take Millie to the park and enjoy the sunshine. It seemed like everyone else had had the same idea, and the place was filled with families feeding the ducks and young couples like ourselves strolling through the neat lawns and formal gardens.

Near the lake, Millie had picked up a scent that intrigued her, and gone after it, snuffling and wheezing in an excited fashion as she tugged at her leash. I'd assumed she could smell one of the squirrels that skittered along the tree branches, so I wasn't quite prepared for what I found when we pushed through the undergrowth into a small, dank clearing. Nothing was happening there, but it was all too obvious that it wasn't long since something had. The earth was tramped down by heavy feet, and wads of discarded tissue lay on the ground, left behind by whoever had been here. The air smelled of sex—a thick, briny odor that couldn't fail to have attracted Millie. Even as I was picking her up so I could carry her out of there, Brett blundered in behind me. Just as I had, he took one look round this tight, sordid space, saw the unmistakable evidence of what had been taking place here, and his eyes widened.

"God, Jenni, how long have we been living in this city, and we had no idea guys came cruising here."

"You think that's what this is?" I wondered how he could be so sure this was a men-only meeting place. After all, I'd heard enough about dogging to know it was an equal-opportunity pursuit.

"Of course. If women were coming here, they'd clean up after themselves, at least." He grinned. "I thought the fact this was men only would appeal to you."

We made our way back out into the fresh air, Millie whining a little at being deprived of all those interesting scents to explore. "Maybe it does," was all I said. "Come on, let's go and get a coffee."

We'd said nothing more about our discovery that afternoon, but Brett had been right. The idea that men were sneaking into those bushes to meet for some kind of sex, whether that was just circle jerks or full-on penetration, did appeal. I'd never been able to explain why, but the thought of guys getting off with each other had always excited me. When Brett and I had discussed our fantasies, though, I'd found it hard to admit to him that I wanted to watch two men having sex. Somehow, it felt strange, taboo. Everyone knew two women pleasuring each other was one of the most popular male fantasies there was—hell, the porn industry pretty much revolved around fulfilling that fantasy. But girls weren't supposed to have any interest in finding out what guys did together, or so I'd always believed.

When I'd finally confessed to Brett that this was what I really wanted, I'd expected him to be alarmed and appalled. He wasn't. In fact, he'd been incredibly sympathetic, all the while explaining that, much as he'd love to help me fulfill that fantasy, he couldn't. He just didn't have a gay bone in his body. He'd done the next best thing, though, buying me a couple of man-on-man porn DVDs that I thought were the closest I'd ever get to watching gay sex in the flesh.

Now, lingering over our breakfast, I let the full implication of Brett's words sink in. There could be only one reason he'd want to go down to the park, and what could be sleazier than sneaking into that sheltered little dogging spot again—particularly if it was occupied at the time we visited?

"Are you serious about this?"

He nodded. "I've been looking on some chat rooms. Seems the park is pretty well known as a pickup spot, but what happens there is mostly spur-of-the-moment stuff. But a handful of guys go down there on Sunday nights who welcome spectators as long as they're discreet."

"Female spectators?" A pulse had started to beat quickly in my pussy at the thought of finally getting to fulfill my fantasy.

"They didn't say, but I reckon if you wear baggy clothes and tuck your hair under a cap, no one will realize."

"You'd do this for me?" Brett even visiting a gay chat room was an eye-opener; the idea that he'd done so purely so he could help give me what I'd always wanted made me want to fling myself across the kitchen table and plant a big, apricot-flavored kiss on his lips.

"For you, Jenni, anything. Now, is there any more coffee in that pot?"

The park was quiet as Brett and I walked, hand in hand, in the direction of the lake. Most of the families had gone home. On one patch of grass near the ornamental gardens, a muscular personal trainer was putting a sweating, red-faced blonde through her paces, barking encouragement as she worked her way through a set of jumping jacks. In less than an hour, dusk would fall and the park gates would be shut for the night.

We'd left Millie at home, snoozing on her favorite cushion in the conservatory. Dogging might have gained its nickname because those who went out to watch others having sex used the excuse of taking their dog for a walk, but if Millie got as excited as she had the last time, she'd surely have advertised our presence. And despite Brett's assurances, I still felt anxious about being a female in this male-only space.

My heart beat faster as we approached the clump of ash trees, their foliage forming a thick canopy that provided perfect shelter from the rest of the park. Brett squeezed my hand, as if sensing my nervousness. In response, I felt my nipples tighten into knots that pressed against the cotton of my shirt. I'd dressed in the most masculine clothes I owned, and hadn't bothered with a bra, but I still felt all too conspicuous as we crept into the undergrowth.

We were in luck. Two men stood in the middle of the clearing, locked in a passionate embrace. Neither of them looked in our direction as we approached. I wasn't sure whether this meant they hadn't heard us, or they were aware of our presence but had decided to ignore us. After all, the men who came here on Sundays advertised for an audience; I was certain they'd be disappointed if they didn't get one.

Brett guided me into a space behind the gnarled trunk of a tree, where we could watch, if not in comfort, at least in a position that offered maximum discretion to the participants—if what they were doing could be called discreet, that was.

Just as on our previous visit, the air was ripe and fuggy, but it wasn't the smell of stale come that made me hold my breath. The men had stepped apart for a moment, and now I got my first proper look at both of them. Older than I'd expected, maybe in their early forties. The bigger, bulkier one had tattoos running the length of both forearms and a piercing in his right eyebrow, while his colleague had black-rimmed glasses and a neatly trimmed goatee. Piercing murmured something to the other man, too low for me to catch, but his command became clear when I saw Goatee reach for the fly of his jeans and undo it.

I had to fight to stifle a gasp when he let his cock flop out into the open. Even half-hard, it was easily the size of Brett's, stiffening and growing further as he wanked it with slow, steady strokes. Piercing seemed just as impressed with it as I was, and I realized in that moment these two guys didn't even know each other, except maybe as screen names in the chat room where they'd arranged this meeting. This was the first time for them, just as it was for me, and hot juice seeped into my panties as I watched them display the goods to each other.

Now Piercing had his cock out. It wasn't long, but it was thick, and like his eyebrow, it had a ring through it. I'd never seen a pierced cock in the flesh before, and I itched to wrap my fingers around it and play with that thick, silver ring, just to see how the guy reacted to the stimulation.

Goatee must have had the same thought, for he stopped playing with his own dick and wrapped his fingers around his friend's instead. Brett, standing close behind me, hugged me and put his mouth to my ear.

"Is this what you wanted to see?" he asked, so softly I could hardly hear him. My reply was a tiny nod of my head. I was too excited to speak, attention focused solely on Goatee's fist as he slid it up and down Piercing's length. His burly companion grunted and returned the favor, closing his thick fingers around his companion's shaft. My panties were so wet they were sticking to my pussy, and I needed to feel a hand between my legs to ease the itch there—mine or Brett's, I didn't really care.

Somehow, I must have communicated my need to him, for he slid a hand down, cupping the denim-covered mound of my pussy with his big palm. Applying a little pressure, he pushed the seam of my jeans against my clit, the friction enough to send delicious tingles of sensation through my cunt. The hard column of his erection pressed against my lower back, but he made no move to free it, or encourage me to do so. He seemed to have decided that this was all about my pleasure, the consummation of a fantasy I'd cherished for so long.

Goatee's fingers were moving in a shuttling rhythm on Piercing's cock, but the stimulation clearly wasn't enough, for he pulled free of the caress and ordered the other man to his knees. I couldn't believe he was going to get down in that mess of wet earth and tissue and god knew what else, but he did. Now his head was on a level with Piercing's crotch, and he didn't need any further instructions. Opening his mouth, he took that thick chunk of meat as far into his throat as he could.

I'd watched this act of oral worship so many times on the DVDs Brett had bought for me, but nothing could compare to seeing it from only a matter of feet away, and hearing the soft gobbling noises Goatee made as he sucked on Piercing's dick. Piercing had his eyes closed and was grunting in satisfaction, occasionally ordering the other man to suck harder, or use his teeth more.

Brett nuzzled at my neck and pressed his hand a little harder into my crotch. I ground myself against his fingers, not caring if a twig snapped beneath my feet or I let out a moan of need. The men in the clearing were too far gone in their own pleasure to hear any noise we made, and I needed to come, desperately.

I couldn't tear my gaze from the erotic tableau they made. Incredibly, Piercing had pushed his cock into Goatee's mouth all the way down to the base. He'd let his jeans fall to just below the hard moons of his buttocks, and Goatee's face was flush against his dark, wiry bush.

"Oh god, yes," he was moaning, repeating the words like a mantra. His hands made tight fists in Goatee's hair, and I reckoned he had to be causing the man some pain as he gripped and tugged. But Goatee just kept on sucking obediently, submissively.

My nipples ached for attention, and I rolled one between my finger and thumb. Brett had undone my jeans, and now his hand slipped below the waistband so he could caress my cunt through my panties. Even though he wasn't touching my clit directly, I felt that extra stimulation in just the right place, keenly, and mewled so loudly I was sure someone would hear me.

I pulled my focus back to the two men in front of me, as Goatee gave a few last, gulping swallows and Piercing came with a roar. Letting his cock slip from Goatee's mouth, the last drops of come falling from its tip to spatter the ground at his feet, he took a step backward. Satisfaction was etched on his craggy features, and I wondered whether he'd just walk away and leave his companion in need of relief. After all, Goatee's cock still stuck out of his fly, red and angry.

But Piercing hadn't quite finished with the humiliation Goatee obviously relished so keenly. A few curt words, and Goatee was back on his feet, cock clenched in his fist once more as he obeyed the order to bring himself to orgasm. From the flush that stained his cheeks, he appeared to be embarrassed that it only took a few strokes to have his come spurting out to join the mess already littering the ground.

Gyrating against Brett's fingers, I felt my own orgasm hit, rolling over me like breakers on a beach. Brett held me until my spasms subsided, murmuring how much he loved me. I couldn't answer him, too overwhelmed by finally having my fantasy brought to life by these two strangers. By the time I opened my eyes again, they'd left the clearing. Probably they'd never meet again, but even if they forgot each other, I knew I would always remember what they'd done together, here in this disreputable corner of an otherwise respectable city park.

"So, did you enjoy that?" Brett asked as I tidied my clothing.

"You bet," I told him. Glancing down, I saw the bulge pressing at the fly of his jeans, and realized he was the only one who hadn't come yet. "Why don't we go home, and I can show you just how much?"

He led me out of the clearing, back into the sweet, clean air of early evening. As we passed the lake, heading back in the direction of the main gates, we passed Goatee, sitting on a bench smoking a cigarette. He looked up, and his eyes met mine. For a moment, I wondered whether he knew we were the ones who'd been watching him. But I saw no sign of recognition in his gaze. Silently, I thanked him for the delicious, sleazy pleasure he'd never know he'd given me, and walked on, my hand clasped tight in Brett's.

THE INSTRUCTOR

Rose de Fer

I'm weightless. Drifting but not falling. Whispers swim around me, but I can't make out the words. Fading. A soft clink. Silverware? Am I in the dining car? There's a faint medicinal smell and I want to leave, but my carriage door won't open. I tug at the handle, irritated. My bracelet is caught. I murmur and twist to pull away, but the delicate chain swells, becoming a manacle around my right wrist. As my eyes flutter open, the dream dissolves around me and I sit up with a gasp.

I'm handcuffed to a bed.

I yank frantically, but the cuffs hold tight—one on my wrist and one on the iron headboard. Wild-eyed, I glance around the room. It's simple, nondescript. Not a hotel. Where the hell am I? I'm no stranger to waking up naked in unfamiliar rooms, but I can usually recall the excesses that led me there. And I'm always free to leave.

I try in vain to pry myself loose, but the unyielding steel ring is too tight even for my tiny wrist to slip out. A cloying unease settles over me and I huddle down under the blanket like a child afraid of the dark. I peer out at my surroundings again, gradually becoming aware of the tall shadow at the foot of the bed. A man is sitting there.

With a cry I clutch the blanket tightly to hide my nakedness. "Who are you?" I demand, trying to keep the tremor out of my voice.

He smiles and rises slowly from his chair, making his way over to me. I'm disturbed by the idea that he might have been sitting there for hours while I slept, watching me as I woke up and strained against the cuffs, waiting like a spider for me to struggle in his web.

Casting my mind back, I can just remember the girl at the bar. The one who gave me that drink. Had I trusted her simply because she was female? More fool me. Reckless, headstrong me.

But something else is fluttering in my memory like a moth against a windowpane. I knew her. Know her. But from where? And where is she now?

"It won't do any good to fight," my captor says calmly. "You'll only hurt yourself."

"Where am I?" He ignores my question and I cower as he stands over me, his nearness a threat. "Have I been arrested?"

He seems amused by my question. "In a manner of speaking."

Kidnapped, then. "Look, my family doesn't have any money."

"That's not what this is about."

Instantly I fear the worst. "Are you going to kill me?" I whisper hoarsely.

"No."

I look into his eyes. They're piercing, glacial. I sense the cruelty he's capable of, but I don't think he's lying.

He watches me watching him, reading my thoughts. I'm a creature of pure fear and helplessness and he knows exactly what to expect from me. I'm not the first he's done this to. The thought makes me shudder.

I don't want to hear the answer, but I can't stop myself asking. "What do you want with me?"

His demeanor changes suddenly. "That is your last question. From now on you will not speak unless you are spoken to. And when you speak, you will address me as 'Sir.' Do you understand?"

My eyes widen, but I don't answer.

Without warning, his hand flashes across my cheek. It's not a hard slap—just hard enough to get my attention.

"Do you understand?"

"Yes," I whisper, cringing. "Sir."

"I'm going to release you now," he says, withdrawing a key from his pocket. "And you're not going to try anything foolish." His cold eyes impart a colder warning.

No, I'm not stupid. My head is still reeling from the madness of the situation. I'll have to play along for now. Bide my time and wait for my moment.

He twists the key in the lock and the cuff springs open, releasing me. I instantly clasp my wrist, rubbing it and glaring reproachfully at him.

"Now I want you to get up and stand in front of the bed, facing me, with your hands on your head. Do it now."

I'm frightened, but I do as he says, covering myself.

"Hands," he instructs firmly.

I summon my boldness, the reckless part of me that's responsible for this situation. I meet his eyes brazenly as I push my breasts together and squeeze them, gyrating like a stripper.

"Is this what you wanna see?" I ask, trying to act unfazed, as though I do this all the time. Lord knows I've bared myself before enough casual partners.

But the icy look he gives me makes me regret the stunt. My bravado evaporates and my hands shake as I lace my fingers and adopt the position he told me to, placing my hands on my head and staring mournfully at the floor.

"I won't see another display of insolence like that," he says coldly. "Will I?"

"No," I whisper.

"No what?"

I swallow. "No, Sir."

The air is heavy with the implicit threat and he lets the silence hang for agonizing seconds while I tremble and wait. At last he speaks again.

"I am the instructor," he says simply. "And you are here to be instructed. Specifically, you are here to be trained to be a slave."

I blink at this bizarre pronouncement.

"Now, then—who am I?" he asks me.

For several moments I'm too bewildered to reply. I keep my eyes on the floor, as though it contains the key to unlocking this mystery. There is something familiar about his voice, his face, but I can't place it. Have I been here before?

"I'll ask you again," he says. His voice is soft, as though this is the most reasonable conversation in the world. "Who am I?"

When I still don't reply he steps nearer and I flinch, fearful of another slap. "The instructor," I say quickly.

"And what is your name, slave?"

"Christine."

Before I can register the movement, he brings his hand down

sharply across my bottom. I yelp, flinging my hands behind me to shield myself. He seizes my arm and holds me firmly, gathering my wrists together in the small of my back. Then, without a word, he spanks me. His hand connects with my tender bottom again and again, making me whimper and struggle. But he holds me fast. I can do nothing but cry out as he rains down a volley of stinging slaps across my cheeks. The punishment lasts a long time, and I am crying long before he is satisfied.

When he releases my wrists I rub the burning flesh of my bottom, then wipe my tear-streaked face, sniffling piteously. In the silence that follows I find myself daring to hope that he will feel bad about how he has treated me, that he will realize I'm not the one he wants for this purpose, that he will let me go.

At the same time I am aware of a strange response within myself. The pain is fading to a tingle that isn't at all unpleasant. In fact, I can feel the warm wetness between my legs as I stand trembling before him, gingerly touching my sore bottom with cool fingertips. If I'm honest with myself, there's something thrilling about actions that have consequences. It's not something I'm used to.

"What is your name?" he asks again.

I open my mouth to speak my name again, but then I shut it just as quickly. That isn't what he wants to hear. I turn my tearful face to look at him and shake my head slightly in confusion, not daring to speak.

Something like a smile softens his features and in a lower voice he asks, "What is your name—slave?"

This time he emphasises the last word and I understand what he wants me to say. He's training me. Conditioning me. I should be outraged but instead I find myself pressing my legs together and after a moment's hesitation I answer, "Slave." Then I add,

"Sir."

"Very good," he says, and I feel oddly uplifted by the pride in his voice. He paces slowly to the center of the room and turns back to face me. "Now, why are you here?"

I force the words out, bewildered by my compliance and yet perversely compelled by his easy control of me. Rebellion simmers just below the surface but his methods are too effective for me to risk defying him. It won't hurt me to say the words if I don't mean them. "To be a slave, Sir."

He praises me like an obedient pupil. "Good girl. Now I want you to put your hands behind your back, wrists crossed. This is First Position."

I do as he says and he continues.

"Turn to face the center of the room, walk five paces, then turn and come back to this spot. Keep your hands in First Position. Now."

The pain is beginning to fade and I am feeling a little bolder but I'm still not brave enough to rebel. I obey the strange command, self-consciously parading myself past him and returning to stand beside the bed.

"Again," he says. "And this time keep your feet along a single line. This will make your hips sway attractively. A good slave must always present herself in a pleasing way for her masters. Hold your head high, but keep your eyes down," he says. "You will not look anyone in the eye unless instructed to. Is that clear?"

"Yes, Sir."

Blushing, I cross the room again as though walking a tight-rope, painfully aware of my nakedness and my vulnerability.

"Very good," he says when I return.

My spirit is returning with every second that the stinging in my bottom fades. I'm burning inside to resist, rebel, but I just don't dare. I'm completely powerless. Could it be there's a part of me that's actually enjoying this?

The instructor stands before me again, and I tremble in anticipation of the next command. So far he's been easy enough to satisfy, but I imagine things can get much worse.

"Place your wrists on top of your head, crossed."

I shudder as the position thrusts my breasts up, arching my back. The exposure is intensely humiliating, but I'm too vulnerable to hold on to my indignation. I simply feel helpless. But at the same time there is something strangely comforting about it. I have the sense that as long as I follow his rules, I will not be harmed. More than that, I will be safe. Protected. Looked after. My sex tingles in response to the thought and I feel my face grow hot. Two sides of me are at war and I'm not at all sure which one is winning.

"This is Second Position," he says. "And now I have another question for you." He looks me in the eye. "Where were you born?"

I feel a sudden pang of longing as I think of my home back in Nevada, deep in the desert, where towering cacti guarded me like sentinels. They're so far away now. I swallow my homesickness and my denial. Things have changed. Forever.

My eyes fill with tears as I give him the answer I know he expects.

"Here, Sir." In admitting it, I am accepting it.

He smiles and praises me, but his voice is a distant murmur through my haze of tears. I sniffle pitifully as my walls begin to crumble.

The instructor lifts his arm slightly, and I flinch away. But he doesn't mean to strike me. He strokes my face and I am so weakened by the show of kindness that I almost wish he would hit me. Chaos is roiling inside my guts, and I can't understand why I'm not fighting. I can't understand why I'm so aroused, why I'm feeling both so rebellious and so obedient.

"Are you afraid of me?" he asks.

"Yes, Sir."

"An honest answer," he says, nodding. "We'll return to that. So far you've done very well. If you continue to do this well you may even earn your new slave name by the end of this training session."

Wiping my eyes, I resist the instinctive urge to feel that that's something I want. He's messing with my mind, but there's no denying the effectiveness of his methods. For a girl who's spent most of her life out of control, following his simple commands to earn praise has shown me that things don't always have to be difficult. The rebel inside me tries to tell me not to take pride or pleasure in these achievements. I'm no one's slave, my bad self insists, and no amount of drilling will turn me into one.

He's watching me and for a moment I wonder if my thoughts are audible to him. Perhaps he simply knows what girls like me think in situations like this. His speeches and questions have a rehearsed quality, as though training slaves is his daily job. I'm both intimidated and excited by that thought.

"Second Position," he says. "Step to the middle of the room."

I obey. Then I gasp when I see the leather wrist cuffs dangling from the ceiling beam. I hadn't noticed them before; my eyes had been on the floor.

As he fastens my wrists into the cuffs he repeats his questions.

"Who am I?"

Now the rebel is silent. My voice quavers as I reply. "The instructor, Sir."

"What is your name?"

"Slave, Sir."

"Why are you here?"

"To be a slave, Sir."

"Where were you born?"

"Here, sir."

"Why are you afraid of me?"

As he asks this I hear a strange sound and when I turn to look, I gasp. He is running the tails of a long leather whip through his fingers. Tears spring to my eyes and I whimper softly, my body trembling. I don't know how to answer. Does he want honesty or some clever interpretation of my situation? I'm afraid to think about it too long, so I blurt out the truth: "Because you control my fate, Sir?"

He nods. "That's true. But it's not the answer I'm looking for. Tell me—do you think this will hurt?" He shows me the whip.

"Yes, Sir," I say, my voice barely a whisper.

"You're right. It will. Do you want me to use it on you?"

"No, Sir."

He closes his eyes and shakes his head, a show of disappointment. Instantly I open my mouth to blurt out the opposite response but he places a finger on my lips, silencing me gently.

"Wrong answer. You are a slave, remember? Your duty is to obey, to give pleasure to your masters. And some masters will take pleasure in whipping you. A good slave will learn to find her own pleasure in the pain."

His hand slips down to my bottom as he lets his words sink in. He gives me a little squeeze, reawakening the sting in my punished cheeks. I whimper, knowing he is right but fearing the reality of it. The pain earlier was terrible at first but it soon shaded into a warm glow. More than that, I actually found it erotic. And as I imagine how much more the whip will hurt I find myself remembering an old fantasy. The memory is patchy but I see myself bound and whipped, rewarded when I am good and punished when I am not. Trained. Disciplined. Controlled. I can even remember describing the fantasy to someone, but I can't make out who it is. My mind is still fuzzy.

The instructor moves behind me and I shudder in anticipation. I was calmer when things were precise and consistent. Now I feel I've been tricked. Or has he merely taken things to the next level, and I'm not keeping up? Tears shimmer in my eyes, turning the room into an underwater blur as I hear the leather tails cut through the air. The lashes slap against my bare back and I yelp, mostly out of surprise. It's not as painful as I'd feared. I relax a little as he plays the whip over my back, making me jump and yelp. But it's bearable. Even strangely calming.

My back is warm when he finally stops, but I'm uninjured. My throat hurts from crying out, however, and he seems to know this.

"Would you like some water?"

"Yes, Sir."

He raises a bottle of water to my lips and begins his question drill again, not feeding me a sip until I've answered. I feel like a lab animal being rewarded for pressing the right buttons. I'm so grateful for the water that I find myself eager to please him. The words have ceased to be humiliating.

When he decides I've had enough he shows me a second whip. This one has much thicker tails and looks far more intense. I know it will hurt.

"Why are you afraid of me?" he asks.

I eye the whip nervously, weighing the implicit threat. Will he thrash me severely this time if I don't give him the right answer? I rack my brain. I can't think what he wants me to say.

"Because you can give me pain without pleasure?" I venture at last.

"A very wise answer," he says, "and true. But still not what I'm looking for."

I'm astonished by my sense of failure, and at the same time I'm disgusted with myself for caring whether he's pleased or not. I only want to go home. But his absolute confidence frightens me. If girls could escape, he wouldn't act as though he knows it's only a matter of time. And why do I want to go home anyway? Something about the association has soured throughout my encounter with this man. This room and this moment feel far more real than my fuzzy memories of "home."

This time the lashes bite deep, making me jump and twist in my bonds. I cry out in pain, straining away from the whip. But I can't get away. Again and again the vicious leather tails slice against my back, setting my tender skin on fire. It crosses my mind that he expects me to find pleasure in this, to take it with grace and dignity. Will he stop if I begin to enjoy it? Even if what he says is true, that just isn't possible. I struggle and cry like a mistreated pet as the lash finds its mark again and again.

He whips me slowly, steadily, impervious to my cries and pleas. It isn't long before I'm sobbing with complete abandon, frightened and in pain. And yet there is something pleasurable in the freedom to scream and struggle like this. All that's expected of me is to suffer. And when I've suffered enough I will answer his questions like a good little girl. He will help me. He will guide me to the right answers and praise me. All I have to do is trust him. Submit. Surrender.

And as the strokes increase in severity the fog in my head begins to clear at last. I remember the girl at the bar, the strange conversation about a life out of control, my unhappiness, the plaintive wish that I could change, a wish that someone could help me. I remember the man she said she worked for, the methods he used. I remember crying in her arms and begging her to take me to him. And I remember agreeing to the drug that would blur my memory and make me forget who I was for a while. It was necessary, she'd said, to ensure that the desire to change came from deep within. Only then could one truly change who one was; only then could the instructor do his job. Only then could fantasy become reality.

The pain comes in waves that wash over me, bright and sharp, soft and sweet. I scream with exquisite release as I give myself over to the possibility that my life could be different. Better. I could let people in, trust them, give myself to them. I let go completely and feel tiny spasms building between my legs. Incredible. I'm going to come.

The change in me must be obvious because the whipping stops. The instructor is beside me now, stroking me, comforting me. I weep in his arms, writhing against him and begging him with my body for what I most need now. My reward. His hands travel down my burning, punished flesh to my bottom, slipping between my cheeks and up between my legs, where I am copiously wet. He presses his fingers against my swollen sex and begins to massage me gently, alternately pinching and stroking my clit.

It only takes a few seconds. The climax hits me like an electric shock. My body leaps and bucks with the force of it but he holds me still, wringing every last jolt of sensation from me until I hang limp in my bonds, gasping and panting, my face soaked with tears.

I am barely aware when he releases me and lets me down. I sink to my knees on the floor in front of him, comforted by the subservient position.

"Look at me," he says softly.

I obey, feeling no sense of shame over anything that's happened. Even my vulnerability feels like strength.

He studies my face and I know another question is coming. "What was your name in your past life?"

My heart twists. I know the answer he wants. Best of all, I know it's true.

Blinking back more tears, I whisper, "I have no past life, Sir."

His eyes crinkle in a smile that moves me to fresh tears. "Good girl," he says with genuine pride. "Very good girl. You've made me very proud, and you've earned your new name."

I lower my head, no longer surprised by my submissive instincts.

"I shall call you Lily."

My eyes shine with tears as I imagine a lonely flower withering in the parched landscape of the desert. Plucked from the wasteland and transplanted to a garden. Blooming.

And as the instructor gathers me in his arms and lets me cry some more, I know that my whole new life is just beginning.

My Pillar-Box Red Cock

Tilly Hunter

When he drops his jeans, bends over and shows me the base of the plug sticking out of his ass, I just can't believe he's been doing this without me—not after what I said that drunken night a few weeks ago. And here I thought he'd called me up to the bedroom to admire our new rug. I heard him vacuuming, ready to roll it out. It's hand woven by Berber nomads, don't you know, one hundred percent wool from Atlas Mountain ewes.

But I'm not admiring the weaving. Instead I'm staring at my husband's ass as he stands on the newly rolled-out rug, having left all his clothes in an untidy pile in one corner of it. I'm staring at the butt plug he's put in his ass. Or rather, it's looking at me, one pearlescent blue pupil surrounded by the iris-like filament of his asshole. It twitches a little, the eye winking out some Morse code that only I can understand. It's saying, "Grab hold of me in your sweaty little fingers, draw me slowly out, stretch his hole with my bulbous girth, push me back in and watch the muscles close, fuck him with me." Oh, I understand exactly what my husband's cheap vinyl butt plug is saying to me.

"So, um, when did you get that?"

"About a fortnight ago." He's still bent over, hands on his knees, craning his neck round to talk to me. "Actually it was twelve days ago, exactly. Which means I'm up to an hour at a time. I started off wearing it for five minutes and increased gradually."

We're standing in our bedroom in broad daylight on a Sunday morning discussing how Ryan has been training his butt for penetration with military precision without telling me. I need to backtrack. Quite far back. I also need to stop staring at the plug and wondering if its round base works as a suction cup.

"Honey, I'm pretty sure you said you didn't want anything near your ass. You do remember that night, right? That's why I haven't mentioned it again."

That night. It was a few weeks ago. Cabernet sauvignon had been on buy-one-get-one-free, so of course we drank both bottles. Then we started talking dirty. "Go on, there must be some fantasy you haven't let on about," I dared him. His turned out to be the relatively mundane one of wanting to watch me with another woman. I'd do it for him, but I was disappointed he came up with something so predictable. He can be pretty filthy at times. But my confession put a bit of a dampener on the evening. He sobered up pretty quick when I said, "I'd really love to fuck your ass with a strap-on."

Oops.

He still doesn't straighten up. He's flaunting that ass at me. And it's the firm, muscular ass of an army PT instructor. "I know what I said."

Yeah, so do I—it was actually a bit more vehement than not wanting anything near his back entry. It had the words *don't, ever* and *fucking well* in it. It left me feeling small and wrong and freakish for putting into words the thing I've pictured over and over in my head. I'd kept it a secret so long, having already discovered his phobia when I tried to run my tongue between his cheeks early on in our relationship.

Ryan stands up at last, moaning a little as the thing shifts inside him. He turns to me and explains himself. The plug is giving his voice an urgent breathlessness, like when you're having to talk to someone but you actually need to dash to the bathroom. "I know what I said and I'm sorry about how it came out. I was drunk; I should have been more sensitive. It was only when I saw how upset you got that I realized it was so important to you. I thought we were just messing around. But then I saw your face. I kept thinking about what you'd said and did a bit of research."

"But why didn't you tell me?"

"I didn't want to get your hopes up. You have to understand that nobody had ever put anything up my ass before; I hadn't even put my own finger up there until three weeks ago. But I did some searches online. Did you know that sixty-three percent of heterosexual couples engage in some kind of anal play?"

"No, I didn't." So now he's the fucking anal oracle or something? I stop myself from pointing out that the stats are probably heavily skewed toward penetration of the female.

"Well, they do. So I started to think maybe there was something in it and started to have a bit of a play. Then I ordered the plugs."

"Plugs?" I emphasize the plural.

"Yeah, I have two more. This is only the small one. I'm not sure about the large one, but I think I'm nearly ready for the medium one."

I want to scream, "Stop right there before I bugger you with a can of deodorant." It's the nearest roughly phallic object I can see. My husband's gotten acquainted with his ass and is talking about butt-plug sizes right in front of me. I want to bend him over and possess him this very instant. I want to pound his butt until his eyes water, force my cock into his tight hole, thrust my hips like a man and give him a damn good seeing to.

"Right. So you've changed your mind?" I'm still not sure if this is going all the way to what my brain thinks is the logical conclusion. I need to hear it. And oh boy, do I hear it.

"Yes, I've changed my mind. I want you to fuck my ass. I thought we could have a look at some strap-ons together and order one."

I'd resigned myself to this being the one fantasy I'd never do. Okay, I mean the one remotely feasible fantasy I'd never do, because I know that a threesome with a multi-tentacled alien ain't happening anytime soon. I thought I'd spend the rest of my life furtively viewing those websites that show bound muscle men getting a good pounding by divine creatures in latex. I already know the strap-on I want, because I've looked. I've compared lengths and girths and colors and quality of fake cocks probably more than I've looked at the real thing. I only had a handful of lovers before I met Ryan in college.

The one I want is pillar-box red. I know it's a cliché, but I want something to contrast nicely with the dark pink of his asshole. Something uncompromisingly bright. The harness is a robust webbing- and padded-plastic affair. The leather and steel ones might look the part, but I bet that leather would stretch. The firm PVC dildo is seven inches long, with a gently shaped head and a subtle flare in girth toward the base. I've even priced it up on different websites, wondering whether to order one just so I can wear it in secret and run my hand up and down my own cock. Sometimes I wonder if I should have been born a boy, but when Ryan fucks me and I feel my pussy clench around his dick I'm more than happy to be a girl. It's just that I want to be fucker as well as fuckee sometimes. Not just on top, but in him.

"How about we try the medium one now? Then we can do some shopping online." I'm going to have to be careful how I introduce him to my chosen strap-on. Even though he's now changed his mind, I fear he'll find my previous research some kind of betrayal.

"Oh wow, I guess we could. I was going to give it a go tomorrow. It's a bit scary-looking, to be honest, even though it's not that much bigger than this one." He delves into the back of his sock drawer and pulls out a drawstring bag. When he turns his back to me to put it on the bed, I get a flash of that blue in his butt and it looks so disgustingly wonderful I want to push him down on his front and take that circle of vinyl in my teeth. I let out a funny little noise and he looks at me with an eyebrow raised as he opens the bag and places two more plugs side by side on the comforter.

One is an absolute monster. I pick it up. It's heavy and more than fills my palm. "Bloody hell, now that one is definitely scary."

"I know. I was a bit horrified when I opened the parcel. But the little one's fine."

I pick up the other one. It's still weighty and a serious size, but not off-the-scale huge. It warms quickly in my hand. I start to imagine sliding it inside him, but I make a spur-of-the-moment decision. "I want to watch you put it in. When we get a strap-on, I want that to be the first time I put something in there. I think it'll be better that way." I can be patient. I can wait so that the first thing I push inside him is my special pillar-box red cock.

Ryan goes to the bathroom to take the other one out, then positions himself kneeling on the bed with a tube of lube and the medium plug. I lean my butt back on a chest of drawers and find that my hips are pulsing just a little inside my slouchy weekend sweatpants. He rubs lube all around his opening, then pushes a finger inside. He spreads more on the plug and presses its tip to his asshole. It is such a sweet sight. And thoroughly obscene. It slides slowly inside as Ryan breathes hard.

"What does it feel like?"

"Big. Fucking big," he murmurs, pausing its inward journey. He gathers himself for the final push. "It feels amazing actually. It's all wrong, something going in when all the muscles want to push it out. But I can't believe how good it feels once you relax around it." His hole is stretching over the widest part and he groans a little as it slips in and settles into place. "The first time I tried, I put my hand on my cock and before I knew it I was coming."

"Come now. Come in me with it in you."

As Sunday mornings go, that one ranks pretty highly. But when the next one rolls around, it's time to up the ante. After he'd fucked me on the new rug, struggling to keep from coming too soon with the object in his ass upsetting his usual equilibrium, I subtly persuaded him about the strap-on we would buy and we placed our order. Two days later, it arrived in a discreet brown parcel. But we decided to wait for the weekend. For Sunday morning, when we have nowhere to be and no visitors expected.

I take the webbing contraption out of its box and work out

the straps, pulling it up my legs, feeding the dildo through the holder and buckling everything into place. I'm otherwise naked but Ryan, sitting on the edge of the bed watching, is mesmerized not by my tits or pussy, but by the red tip of my cock. I stroke my hand up the shaft and his feet fidget. I step up to him and thrust it toward his face. He leans down and puts his lips around the end. Instant power. I want to push it down his throat until he gags.

"I'm going to fuck you senseless," I tell him while it's deep inside his mouth. He moans his assent and then his disappointment as I pull it out. "On your knees on the rug."

He hesitates before sliding down onto the floor. For a moment I think he's going to say something. Does he want to make a speech to mark this momentous occasion? Or express last-minute doubts? I want to thrust it in him so quickly he can't change his mind. But I need to make sure he's sure. If he changes his mind, I'll just have to live with it. My fantasy has only recently become his and it would be quite reasonable for him to have second thoughts.

I kneel behind him. "Are you okay with this?"

He's on all fours on the rug and when he turns his head to me it's just like that first time I saw the plug in his butt. But this time his voice is less assured. "I'm a little, um, apprehensive. Yeah, that's the word. Part of me is wondering how the hell I got myself into this position."

"The dildo is slightly narrower than the medium plug," I assure him. "I'm going to take it very slowly, and it's not going to hurt." He's been wearing the medium plug every evening since last Sunday.

"Just be gentle," he says. "It's one thing putting a plug in yourself. Letting someone else fuck you..." He trails off.

"I'll be gentle." I want to say something momentous myself. That I'm honored to be popping his ass cherry, perhaps. But I don't want him to get any more worked up. I squirt lube into my hand and massage it all over my dick. I place my hands lightly on his asscheeks to begin with, then start to circle my thumbs into his crack, spreading more lube toward his hole. I've spent the last week picturing to myself what it's going to look like when I press the tip of my cock to that puckered hole and ease it inside him. And now I'm so close to fulfillment. My throat is tight and my pussy is wet.

It's not just that he's handing me control and letting me play out my fantasy on him. It's the fact that he wants it. He's offering himself up to me in the most intimate way possible, and I can see from his eyes that he wants it as badly as I do. That look powers all the way to the muscles I'll be using to thrust inside him.

When I've spread the lube all around him, I slip the tip of a finger inside, waiting for his sphincter to relax and let me in. I slide it in and out, easing him open, and push in a second finger. He rocks his hips back onto me, breathing hard. His back and butt are damp with sweat already. Inside, his ass is hot and moist with a texture I know only from the times I've stretched to put a finger an inch up my own butt while masturbating. That damp, woolly feel. I'm already awed at having my sensitive fingertips pressed inside my husband, but it's time to put my cock in there. I slide my fingers out.

"Part your legs a little." I can't reach otherwise. I have to kneel high to bring the tip to the right place. He's suddenly desperate, skittish, squirming into position too quickly, turning to try to grasp the dildo and pull it into himself. I place a hand on his hip. "Relax."

The butt plugs have paid off. I push my cock against him and I see his ring loosen and push outward as he opens up for me. The shaped head disappears inside. I realize I'm holding my breath and let it out as I ease the shaft gradually in. Just once, Ryan's ass tightens and his shoulders tense. I see the rug wrinkle as he grasps it. But he calms himself and starts to moan low with each out-breath.

The flared shaft stretches his hole wider, excess lube rippling at his opening as his taut skin skims it off the dildo's surface. I'm panting as I push in the final inch and rest the strap-on's frame against his body. "I'm all the way in."

It's Ryan's turn to let out a trapped lungful of air. He drops his head toward the rug, accentuating the animal strength of his shoulders. I pull my cock slowly back until I see the beginning of the head one inch from the end. I slide it back in and begin to fuck him slowly. I watch the thin, wrinkled skin of his asshole glide in and out along the dildo. I've imagined what this moment was going to feel like, but am completely unprepared for the intensity of the experience. He's mine. I've bent him over and penetrated him and now I'm going to fuck his brains out. I have my cock deep inside him, pounding him, and from the sounds he's making, he's loving it.

He rocks his ass in time to the fucking, slamming up into the base of the dildo, inviting it to hammer into him harder and faster. I grasp his hips tightly to help me pound him deeper. I'm hot and sweating from the exertion. Webbing teases my labia and rubs my own asscheeks. My thighs ache and my knees are getting stiff.

Ryan's moans change. He's struggling to say something, muffled against his forearm. "I...I..." I smile at the realization that I'm fucking him into incoherence. "I'm going to come," he eventually stammers out. I only hear the *F* of the next word, as a deep groan of satisfaction rips the curse from his throat. I can't see his cock, but as that groan tails off I know it's time to slow down. I come to a rest halfway in.

"Fuck." He eventually manages to complete the word.

"Yes," I agree, my hands resting on the top curve of his butt. "Fuck."

I let him catch his breath. "I'm going to come out now," I say. "Breathe deep for me." As he sighs, I pull my cock out, watching his hole tighten over the tip and pulse as it empties.

I stand and slip off the straps, kicking them over my feet. Ryan hasn't moved. I sit down beside him and let him rest his head on my thigh. "Honey," I say, "You've come on our new rug. Hand woven by Berber nomads. It's one hundred percent wool. Dry-clean only."

Ryan looks up at me without raising his head, like he's completely spent. "I honestly couldn't give a shit right now if it was hand woven from moon dust by little green men."

I watch the puddle of come slowly sink into the wool, knowing that a quick dash for a towel could mop up the worst before it's all absorbed. It's only a rug.

A First Time for
Everything

Rachel Kramer Bussel

$\mathcal{A}$ re you sure you want to do this?" Chip asked me.

"As sure as I'll ever be," I said, feeling surer even as the words came out of my mouth. After all, what kind of a tease would I be if I backed out of the bukkake party I'd organized myself?

It all started with truth or dare. I'm a wordy girl and will always pick truth over dare, even though I consider myself pretty gutsy. But without truth, without words, without sylla bles spilling out into sentences, dares don't make any sense; they're just reckless actions of the sort performed by drunk boys in late-night race cars, rather than the magnificent grace of a tightrope walker or bungee jumper. I want to be the dare-devil superhero girl of sex, boldly going where few, if any, of my peers have gone before. If I go with a dare, it's of my own making, one that really does push me right up to my limits, not just where an envious partygoer would like to see me go.

The truth is, I'm a thrill-seeker. I'm the girl who's been there, done that, and gone on to relish telling the story over and over again. I've had sex with men and women, in groups, in public, in dungeons. I've had all manner of sex toys, real and improvised, shoved into my pussy. I've been fucked underwater and spanked on camera. I've said yes to things simply to shock other people. I've used a violet wand and a Magic Wand and a TENS Unit. I've had all my toes shoved into a greedy bottom's mouth, and much more. I've made a girl profess her love to me the first night I met her, all because of the way I wielded my fist.

I'm only twenty-four, but let's just say I get around. I prefer being single because it gives me room to play the field without worrying about hurting anyone's feelings. I like coming home at six a.m. once in a while, doing the quick two-hour catnap, shower and change, using the memory of the night before to fuel me when the lack of sleep threatens to kick in. I'm the one my friends call on for advice, even referring me around to curious but shy friends: "Oh, call Caitlin, she'll know." Yes, that's me, the girl who's done just about everything (and everyone), whose little black book is actually a massive journal scrawled with names and stories and phone numbers and Polaroids, a glorious jumble of limbs and cocks and breasts and lips, ones I've never sought to try to untangle into a neat, tidy chronological history.

Sex has always been the starting point, never the end, to any inquiry about who I am. It's the gateway drug to, well, more sex, to finding out more about how I operate, what buttons I like having pushed and which I set permanently to caution. This utterly carnal lifestyle is balanced by the hours, days, weeks, years of fantasies that must jumble together until I'm compelled to act. I'm not just an ethical slut, I'm a thoughtful one, too. The time I spend thinking about sex, pondering its every nuance and possibility, far exceeds the time I spend engaging in it, and

I'm perfectly happy with that uneven ratio.

So when Sally asked me what my deepest, dirtiest, darkest fantasy was during what had, up till that point, been a rather tepid game of truth or dare (bra size and taking one big bite of everything in the refrigerator amongst the highlights), I told her—and the whole room. "I want to do bukkake. I mean, be on the receiving end. I want to be lying naked on the floor and see a circle of cocks, all pointing at me. I want a round of boys to want me so badly they'll get naked in front of each other, press their dicks up in my face, while I beg them to come all over me. I want them to take turns shoving their cocks down my throat, slapping them against my lips, rubbing them on my skin, in my hair, doing whatever the hell they please. Maybe I'll be tied up, though then that would deprive me of the pleasure of giving two hand jobs at once. I don't know exactly how it would work, but it's been a mainstay of my fantasy life for years." I paused, mentally highlighting the vision in my mind where they all started to spurt at once, barely giving me a chance to open up and say, "Aaah." I swallowed hard and blinked rapidly, trying to get back into the present. "Yeah," I finished quietly, breathless, my eyes closed, almost ready to cry. Some fantasies are too primal, too out there, too real to ever admit—even to ourselves. But it was true; just thinking about all those anonymous cocks close enough to taste, close enough to smell, close enough to swallow, had my panties soaking.

I wasn't the only one who was intrigued with the idea. Everyone started asking me logistical questions, their eyes lit up, the tension in the room palpable, but I shushed them. "It's just a fantasy. You asked for the truth and you got it. If you really want me to go through with it, catch me next time I say 'dare.'"

I didn't mean to sound so haughty, but then again, I hadn't meant to reveal something so intimate when everyone else was only sharing the most superficial of details. I hugged my arms to myself, beyond blushing. What does it say about a girl that she dreams of jizz raining down on her face, dreams of being a sex object in the most extreme fashion in the way that some girls dream of getting married? What does it say about me that after I went home, the idea just wouldn't go away? I'd thought it was one of those fantasies that could never come true, and even if it could, that would be pushing things, even for me. Whoever heard of women willingly submitting to bukkake outside of porn? Maybe gay men, but that was okay. They'd be pigs amongst pigs (in the best possible sense of the word, of course). But who would I be in such a scenario? Could I ask men to degrade me and respect me and get off on me, literally, all at the same time?

Apparently, I could, because my gay friend Chip called me the next day and tried to sound casual about bringing it up. "God, Caitlin, when you said that, everyone in the room got a hard-on. Even Mikki," he said, referencing our most vanilla, conservative friend, who just happened to be a lesbian (but would never call herself a dyke). "Seriously. It wasn't just that we were getting off on the idea, but your voice got so breathy when you said it, like you were literally seeing yourself doing it in your head, not just spouting off some story you tell all the time to impress people."

"Thanks, I guess," I said, wondering what kind of can of worms I'd opened up. "But it's nothing, really. It's a fantasy."

"But what if...?" His voice trailed off.

"What if *what?*" I hissed.

"What if you could actually do it? What if I found you hot, straight guys—big cocks guaranteed—who were into it? I'd so do that for you. All I'd ask is that I get to watch."

"Whoa, whoa, whoa...slow down there. You? Watching me? And where would these guys come from?" I was supposed to be suspicious, supposed to protest, but I was intrigued and knew from the pounding in my pussy I wasn't going to block the thoroughly filthy path this conversation had started down.

"I know people, Cait, guys who'd love to jerk off over your pretty face."

"Like who?" I just couldn't imagine anyone we know would actually volunteer for such a task, in the presence of other guys.

"Rob, for one."

"Rob? Hot Rob? Really?" My nipples hardened at the thought of bodybuilder Rob, always so brooding, silent and hunky, being naked before me. I'd tried flirting with him in the past but he seemed so stiff and quiet.

"Yes, Rob, I already asked," he said.

"What?" The word came out as a yell, but inside, I was starting to get totally wet.

"And Rob can bring Jeremy and he said he has at least two other friends who are interested. They've all been tested and are single, so there'll be no jealous girlfriends butting in. And I have another friend, Omar, who wants in on it. I'll arrange everything; you just have to show up."

"Really? You'd do that for me? I mean..." I trailed off, not really sure what I meant since I'd never been in a situation remotely like this one before.

"Really, Cait, trust me. And it's not for you. Well, it is, but it's for us, too. Believe me." We hung up and I slid beneath my quilt, letting my fingers plunge deep inside my wetness as I contemplated saying yes to making my fantasy come true. The answer was obvious.

I wound up letting Chip plan the whole thing, and when he was done, in a week's time, he had five guys willing and eager to cover me in their come. It wasn't quite the dozen-man orgy of dick I'd fantasized about, but the fact is, we live in New York, and a twelve-cock circle jerk along with spectators, and me, would probably have been too much to ask for. Five was manageable, a nice, albeit odd number, just slightly above four, which was still a respectable configuration. What we were about to embark on could even be called a five-some, if that were a word, I told myself, and then Chip. "Caitlin, let's just face it. This is your big slutty night. Whether it's five or fifty cocks, it's still bukkake. Be proud, girl! Everyone I've told about this is totally jealous. You're gonna have the time of your life; don't downplay it. This is your chance to live out a fantasy you never thought you'd get to." He was right. As his words burned in my ears, I went about cleaning up for what promised to be the party to end all parties. I had a few days, but I'd need them.

The night of the party, I was the perfect host. I prepared a spread of hors d'oeuvres, light snacks like veggies and fruit, some chips, some candy, and laid out soft drinks and a few beers, though I kept the alcohol light. I offered plenty of lube, flavored and not, condoms, in case one thing led to another, and some sex toys, including handcuffs. I'd thrown in the restraints I sometimes get shackled to my headboard with. Yes, I'd decided to do it where I'd be most comfortable, on my bed. Chip was there to oversee things and to get off on the spectacle. "What about this?" he asked, rummaging through my toy chest as only a gay man can, coming up with a red blindfold my ex had gotten me years ago. I didn't even know I still had it.

"But I want to *see* all those cocks," I said, already picturing them wanking away just for me. That was the part I liked the best; the men wouldn't just be jerking off, they'd be doing it with a purpose. I'd be the center of attention *and* get to feel wave after wave of hot come splashing across my face. I'd always loved the depravity of shutting my eyes and submitting to that most intense of sensations. Even more than swallowing a lover's spunk, having him grace my cheeks, lips, even my hair with it, made me feel at once worthy and degraded. I'd had lovers refuse to do it, unable to see me as the filthy whore I sometimes longed to be. One ex had chickened out at the last minute, able to paint my breasts creamy white but otherwise only wanting to come on my insides, not my outsides. Knowing that men were being hand-picked for this activity, men who'd want to be there, who'd know just how much I wanted it, was a truly special thing to contemplate. Utterly perverse, utterly fucked up and utterly arousing all at once, all the more so because they weren't just horny beasts off the street, but men I admired and respected enough to welcome into my home to defile me. Unless you know the thrill of pure submission, those two things may sound like opposites, but believe me, they're not. It takes a special, enlightened, intelligent kind of man to treat a slutty girl like me just right.

"Well, I'd recommend keeping the blindfold handy, both for you and for them. They may not be able to go through with it with you staring up at them. Plus think about how your other senses will be enhanced by not being able to see." I shut my eyes and pictured myself surrounded by cock, pure cock. We were expecting the five guests who'd RSVPed, so that would be five sets of dicks, five sets of balls, and hopefully five hot blasts of come streaming over my lips and the rest of my face. It was like a gang bang, but even better.

"Okay," I whispered, already feeling my body respond to the mere thought with an intense ache.

What does a girl wear to her very own bukkake party? I pondered, flipping through my closet and then my dresser drawers. Nothing seemed quite right, considering, but I didn't want to answer the door naked. I settled for a simple, sheer nightie in mint green, and almost as soon as I'd put it on, the doorbell rang. Chip had been urging me away from my makeup, against my natural instincts (how could I host a party with a bare face?), but now the doorbell had decided it.

The first guest to arrive was hot Rob, wearing basic jeans, sneakers and a white T-shirt. He'd brought a friend who could've been his twin. Both were equally delectable.

"Welcome," I said, giving a small smile to the newcomer and a flirty wink to Rob. "I'm Caitlin," I said, sticking out my hand.

"Joe," he said, reaching forward and enveloping me in a hug. My body responded to his sheer size, and I wondered if his cock would match his heft.

Rob seemed to want in on the hugging action, and as soon as Joe put me down, he swept me up. "You look beautiful tonight, Caitlin," he said, possibly the longest sentence he'd ever bestowed on me.

"Rob," I said, smirking slightly. "You don't have to butter me up, you know, I'm a sure thing, tonight, anyway."

"Look, I know that. And if you want the truth, I'm a little nervous. I've never been in a room full of cocks before."

"Well, if it makes you feel any better, neither have I," I said.

Well, that wasn't strictly true; I'd been to orgies and sex parties where naked couples abounded, but none where dick would be so close to dick and I couldn't wait. "And...I've been especially looking forward to seeing what you've got under there," I said to him, lightly running my fingers over his package. He stirred beneath my touch and as a reward, I lowered the nightie so my boobs popped out. Rob leaned down and began sucking one nipple while I moaned. The doorbell rang, but I figured someone else would get it. I wasn't sure about proper bukkake party etiquette, but that seemed like an oxymoron if I'd ever heard one!

We continued to kiss and fondle each other and I just shut my eyes and focused on Rob. That lasted all of a minute or two until Chip was pulling me aside. "Save some room for the main course," he whispered. I giggled, then winked at him as I twirled around, before clapping my hands and calling everyone to attention.

"Okay, boys, I guess we're ready to get started. I just wanted to thank you all for coming (ahem) and tell you how excited I am." With that I paused and made eye contact with each of the men whose cocks were soon going to be right up in my face. "The only rule I have tonight is that we're all here to have fun, and I want to make sure you're all comfortable. Does anyone have any questions?"

One guy, Jaime, raised his hand. "Can we come any time we want?"

This was something I hadn't considered; I'd sort of assumed that they'd all jointly have the urge to splatter me with their jism...just like in the movies. But the question also granted me the power to answer, and thereby control his orgasm, and my pussy responded to this unexpected opportunity. "No." I looked directly into his eyes, then walked toward him, reaching under his shirt to twist his nipple. He whimpered, and I smiled. "No, Jaime, you're all going to come when I tell you to. Just because I'll be lying there aching to suck, lick and feel your cocks, doesn't mean I'm not in charge. If you want to stay at the party, you'll have to learn to wait."

The collective mood in the room went from excited to practically orgasmic as we all realized that this wasn't a prank, but that we were all about to engage in something we'd only dreamed of. "Okay, then, I'll give you a few minutes to get naked. I'll be right over here," I said, pointing to my room. I wasn't sure how they wanted to handle that process, so I let them be while I slipped out of my lingerie and looked down at my naked body. The slight curve to my belly felt sexy, and I slid my hand down over it to my mound, which sported just a few tufts of pubic hair.

I walked over to my bed, the scene of the crime, as it were, and lay down on my back. Chip placed the blindfold and a bottle of water near me, then kissed me on the cheek. "All those cocks are soon to be yours," he whispered to me, and I opened my eyes long enough to see that his own cock was extremely aroused. I began playing with myself, lightly stroking my clit, then running a finger along my slit, trying to be patient. Once the naked men had trouped in and I glanced at them as a group, they ceased to be individuals distinguishable by voice and looks and conversation. They were all equal, their cocks together forming a whole that would transport me into another dimension, or so it felt. I let myself sink fully into that fantasy, losing whatever shreds of propriety I was clinging to in order to make the most of this momentous opportunity, for that is what it was.

The first man to saunter over was Jaime, and I immediately felt a frisson of arousal as I looked at his cock. It was already hard, and it was fat and delicious looking. I smiled at him, then rolled over to the edge of the bed, turned onto my side and brought my mouth within sucking distance by way of greeting.

Without saying a word, he offered me his dick. Well, the head of it, anyway. His fist was wrapped around it and he fed it to me slowly. As I took the rounded tip in, then let my lips move down over the crown, I shuddered. Nothing makes me more aroused than wrapping my mouth around a man's hard cock. Today it didn't matter whose cock it was or what he thought of me or even how he was feeling. For once, it was okay for it to be All About Me, though I was sure the men would enjoy themselves as well. I immediately had to keep stroking myself as I swallowed Jaime's cock, his hardness making me frantic. Before I could really start bucking up and down though, he wrapped his fingers in my hair and pulled me away. His forcefulness combined with my now-empty mouth turned me on even more.

"Baby...if you don't want me to come, you can't suck me like that. I'm only a man, after all," he said, taking a step back. I looked up at him, begging with my eyes, running my tongue over my lips, but he shook his head, seeming to take delight in withholding it. "Later," he murmured, and when I turned onto my back, I saw that another man was next to him and three more on my other side, perched on the bed so they could be close enough. They were each stroking their cocks, almost tentatively, as if waiting for a cue from their comrades that they could go faster. I'd given up trying to distinguish whose cock was whose, because at that moment, it just didn't matter.

I moved so I was facing the trio, my back toward Jamie and

his pal. I opened my mouth and two men brushed their cocks against my tongue. I looked up and all I saw was dick, dick, dick, literally, as another one appeared near the others, trying to get inside, though as talented a fellatrix as I am, that would've been impossible. I could hear heavy breathing and pumping on the other side and Chip clapping in delight. "Give it to me," I said, stretching my mouth as wide as I could so those first two cockheads could fully enter my mouth.

This was much farther than I'd ever gone before, for even the largest cock I'd swallowed, and there were some that had made me truly stretch my mouth, gag and strain, didn't come close to having two dicks jockeying for position. Soon I pulled back and kissed the three tips. I took the dildo I'd placed beside me and began working it into my pussy. I had lube nearby, too, but found that I didn't need it. I knew this wasn't the traditional version of this kind of gang bang, where the men's pleasure was paramount, but since I'd orchestrated this scenario, I wanted to reap the rewards. Far from being humiliated, I was overjoyed at getting to arrange this affair to my exact specifications, and the wetness I found between my legs proved it.

I was torn between closing my eyes and focusing on the feel and smell of so many cocks and seeing them in action. I sat up on one elbow, dildo inside me, and we all jerked off communally, grunting and grinding, hands flying over skin, slamming and jerking, violent words for harsh actions yielding dizzying results. I'd always found it to be true that a light touch may as well be a tickle; I need firm, steady pressure, and gazing upon these men with cocks in fists, it was apparent to me that they did, too.

Under my observation, the men seemed to jerk their cocks faster, moving in sync. Someone crawled behind me and

I lowered my head down to the sheet so his penis could rub against my forehead. That gave the others entrée to slide closer, hover directly on top of me and slap their dicks against my face. I fucked myself with the dildo, wishing I had a vibrator because soon my hips were rising and crashing down against the mattress, my eyes tearing in ecstasy as all those penises suffused my senses. I turned my face slightly to the left and took the nearest dick into my mouth, easily swallowing its long, swollen length. Just then, I felt the first jet of cream land on my back, and I whimpered as best I could with a mouth full of cock. I looked up into the eyes of Rob, and he cradled the back of my head gently in his hand as I sucked him. This may sound crazy, but it felt spiritual to me, a moment of bonding that went far beyond the mechanics of sex. Or maybe I'm just the rare girl who can have a holy moment with five gorgeous cocks surrounding her.

I gave everything I had to Rob, slamming the dildo so deep inside me it bordered on pain, the best kind of pain, as I let him invade my mouth. I'd wanted this invasion, asked for it, negotiated it, and now I delighted in it, all of it. I moaned against his mouth, urging him to come down my throat, and my man of the moment obliged. The stream of hot liquid surged into my mouth and I swallowed, my cunt contracting around the dildo at the same time. Rob's release freed me to lean back and simply let the men take over. I surrendered to the glory of this unique situation and watched as one, then another, then yet another dick let loose until I was coated in sticky, white, beautiful come. I reached up and smeared it all over my face, and kissed whoever's lips moved forward to kiss mine. I didn't want to get up just yet; this sex spell was too beautiful to be broken. I lay there and smiled up at my suitors, my good-time guys, my bukkake boys, a grin covered with come, basking in pure bliss. It sure beat the hell out of most of my other sexual firsts. Chip winked at me, and I winked right back, reaching out my hands for whoever wanted to grab them.

About
the Authors

VALERIE ALEXANDER lives in Arizona. Her work has been previously published in *Best of Best Women's Erotica, Best Bondage Erotica* and other anthologies.

JACQUELINE APPLEBEE (writteninshadows.wordpress.com) is a British writer who breaks down barriers with smut. Jacqueline's stories have appeared in various anthologies including *Best Women's Erotica, Ultimate Lesbian Erotica, Penthouse* and *DIVA* magazine. Jacqueline has also penned *An Expanded Love*, a romance about multiple loving.

OLIVIA ARCHER (archerserotica.com) is your typical California girl. That is, if your definition of "typical" includes writing porn by the pool under a hot Hollywood sun. Her stories have appeared in *Frenzy: 60 Stories of Sudden Sex* and *Women in Lust: Erotic Stories*.

ERZABET BISHOP has been crafting stories since she could first pound keys on her parents' old typewriter. She is a contributing author to *Milk & Cookies & Handcuffs, Smut by the Sea V2* and *Coming Together: Hungry for Love*. She is the author of the *Erotic Pagans Series: Beltane Fires*.

GRETA CHRISTINA has been writing professionally since 1989. She is author of *Bending: Dirty Kinky Stories About Pain, Power, Religion, Unicorns, & More*, and *Why Are You Atheists So Angry? 99 Things That Piss Off the Godless*. Her writing has appeared in multiple newspapers, magazines and anthologies, including three volumes of *Best American Erotica*.

ELIZABETH COLDWELL lives and writes in London. Her stories have appeared in anthologies including *Anything for You, Cheeky Spanking Stories* and *Fast Girls*. She can be found at The (Really) Naughty Corner, elizabethcoldwell.wordpress.com.

DELOVELYOLIVE is an avid reader, writer and reviewer of erotic literature. She currently resides in the United States with her husband and three children. Her favorite types of stories to read are unique, heartfelt and embrace the ideals of a sex-positive culture.

JOCELYN DEX shares her home with a six-four alpha male and varying numbers of spoiled cats and dogs. She currently writes erotic paranormal romance about Sempire Demons for Ellora's Cave Publishing. She believes in hot sex and happily-ever-afters. Visit her at jocelyndex.com to find out what a Sempire Demon is.

ROSE DE FER loves the view from the edge. Her writing often explores themes of bondage, D/s, petplay and paranormal romance. Her stories appear in *Red Velvet and Absinthe,* the forthcoming *Darker Edge of Desire* and numerous Mischief anthologies including *Underworlds, Submission* and *Forever Bound.* She lives in England.

JEREMY EDWARDS is the author of the erotocomedic novels *Rock My Socks Off* and *The Pleasure Dial.* His short stories have appeared in over fifty anthologies, including four volumes in *The Mammoth Book of Best New Erotica* series. Readers can surprise him in his underwear at jeremyedwarderotica.com.

BREN EMILE has been writing ever since her chubby fingers could wrap around a pen (well, she went through a phase where she just chewed the pens for a while, but eventually she graduated to prose). She's involved in theater and lives in the Twin Cities.

BRANDY FOX writes poetry, stories, essays and novels for both children and adults. Her erotica appears in *Women in Lust* and *The Mammoth Book of Quick and Dirty Erotica.* She lives in Washington State with her spouse, children, and a garden with all the organic produce and eggs she desires.

KATYA HARRIS lives in Kent in the United Kingdom with her boyfriend, daughter and three crazy rat boys. You can find her on Twitter @Katya_Harris and on Facebook. She hopes that you like what she's written and that you'll come back for more.

TILLY HUNTER (tillyhuntererotica.blogspot.co.uk) is a British author with a wicked imagination and a taste for quirky erotica.

She has stories in anthologies from Xcite Books, MLR Press, House of Erotica and others. Her first solo ebook, *Miranda's Tempest: Three Classic Tales with a Kinky Twist*, is out now.

D. L. KING (dlkingerotica.blogspot.com) is the editor of anthologies such as *Slave Girls, Under Her Thumb* and *The Harder She Comes,* winner of the Lambda Literary Award and the Independent Publisher Book Award gold medal. Her stories can be found in *Best Bondage Erotica, Anything For You* and *Luscious,* among others.

JESSICA LENNOX's erotic work can be found in *Anything Goes: Queer Lesbian Erotica; Curvy Girls; Girl Fever; Spank!; Where the Girls Are; Hurts So Good: Unrestrained Erotica; Rubber Sex* and *Best Women's Erotica 2008.*

Writing under her pen name, **JAYE MARKHAM** lives in the Florida Panhandle where she is working on a lesbian romance novel. She has always admired the women who have served our country as Secretary of State. This is her fantasy of how she would have offered her service.

TIFFANY REISZ is the international bestselling author of the darkly comic Gothic erotica series *The Original Sinners,* a genre she made up entirely on her own. Tiffany lives in Portland, Oregon, with her boyfriend, her cats and her delusions of grandeur.

GISELLE RENARDE is a queer Canadian, avid volunteer, contributor to more than one hundred short-story anthologies, and author of books like *Anonymous, The Red Satin Collection* and *My Mistress' Thighs*. Ms. Renarde lives across from a park with two bilingual cats who sleep on her head.

JADE A. WATERS (jadeawaters.com) began her literary naughtiness when she convinced her boyfriend that the sexiest form of foreplay was reading provocative synonyms from a thesaurus. Her latest piece, "The Flogger," can be found in *The Big Book of Orgasms* from Cleis Press.

About the Editor

RACHEL KRAMER BUSSEL (rachelkramerbussel.com) is a New Jersey-based author, editor and blogger. She has edited over fifty books of erotica, including *Anything for You: Erotica for Kinky Couples; The Big Book of Orgasms; The Big Book of Submission; Baby Got Back: Anal Erotica; Suite Encounters; Going Down; Irresistible; Gotta Have It; Obsessed; Women in Lust; Surrender; Orgasmic; Cheeky Spanking Stories; Bottoms Up; Spanked: Red-Cheeked Erotica; Fast Girls; Flying High: Sexy Stories from the Mile High Club; Do Not Disturb; Going Down; Tasting Him; Tasting Her; Please, Sir; Please, Ma'am; He's on Top; She's on Top; Caught Looking; Hide and Seek,* and is *Best Bondage Erotica* series editor. Her anthologies have won eight IPPY (Independent Publisher) Awards, and *Surrender* won the National Leather Association Samois Anthology Award. Her work has been published in over one hundred anthologies, including *Best American Erotica 2004* and *2006.* She wrote the popular "Lusty Lady" column for the *Village Voice.*

Rachel has written for *AVN, Bust,* Cleansheets.com, *Cosmopolitan, Curve,* The Daily Beast, Elle.com, TheFrisky.com, *Glamour, Harper's Bazaar,* Huffington Post, *Inked,* Mediabistro, *Newsday, New York Post, New York Observer, Penthouse,* The Root, Salon, *San Francisco Chronicle, Time Out New York* and *Zink,* among others. She has appeared on "The Gayle King Show," "The Martha Stewart Show," "The Berman and Berman Show," NY1 and Showtime's "Family Business." She hosted the popular In the Flesh Erotic Reading Series, featuring readers from Susie Bright to Zane, and speaks at conferences, does readings and teaches erotic writing workshops across the country. She blogs at lustylady.blogspot.com.

Red Hot Erotic Romance

Obsessed
Erotic Romance for Women
Edited by Rachel Kramer Bussel

These stories sizzle with the kind of obsession that is fueled by our deepest desires, the ones that hold couples together, the ones that haunt us and don't let go. Whether just-blooming passions, rekindled sparks or reinvented relationships, these lovers put the object of their obsession first.
ISBN 978-1-57344-718-8 $14.95

Passion
Erotic Romance for Women
Edited by Rachel Kramer Bussel

Love and sex have always been intimately intertwined—and *Passion* shows just how delicious the possibilities are when they mingle in this sensual collection edited by award-winning author Rachel Kramer Bussel.
ISBN 978-1-57344-415-6 $14.95

Girls Who Bite
Lesbian Vampire Erotica
Edited by Delilah Devlin

Bestselling romance writer Delilah Devlin and her contributors add fresh girl-on-girl blood to the pantheon of the paranormal. The stories in *Girls Who Bite* are varied, unexpected, and soul-scorching.
ISBN 978-1-57344-715-7 $14.95

Irresistible
Erotic Romance for Couples
Edited by Rachel Kramer Bussel

This prolific editor has gathered the most popular fantasies and created a sizzling, no-holds-barred collection of explicit encounters in which couples turn their deepest desires into reality.
978-1-57344-762-1 $14.95

Heat Wave
Hot, Hot, Hot Erotica
Edited by Alison Tyler

What could be sexier or more seductive than bare, sun-warmed skin? Bestselling erotica author Alison Tyler gathers explicit stories of summer sex bursting with the sweet eroticism of swimsuits, sprinklers, and ripe strawberries.
ISBN 978-1-57344-710-2 $15.95

Happy Endings Forever and Ever

Try This at Home!

Morning, Noon and Night
Erotica for Couples
Edited by Alison Tyler

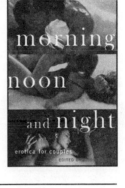

Alison Tyler thinks about sex twenty-four hours a day, and the result is *Morning, Noon and Night*, a sizzling collection of headily sensual stories featuring couples whose love fuels their lust. From delicious trysts at dawn to naughty nooners, afternoon delights and all-night-long lovemaking sessions, Alison Tyler is your guide to sultry, slippery sex.
ISBN 978-1-57344-821-5 $15.95

Anything for You
Erotica for Kinky Couples
Edited by Rachel Kramer Bussel

Whether you are a BDSM aficionado or a novice newly discovering the joys of tying up your lover, *Anything for You* will unravel a world of obsessive passion, the kind that lies just beneath the skin.
ISBN 978-1-57344-813-0 $15.95

Sweet Danger
Erotic Stories of Forbidden Desire for Couples
Edited by Violet Blue

Sweet Danger will inspire you with stories of a sexy video shoot, a rough-trade gang bang, a public sex romp served with a side of exquisite humiliation and much, much more. What is *your* deepest, most sweetly dangerous fantasy?
ISBN 978-1-57344-648-8 $14.95

Irresistible
Erotic Romance for Couples
Edited by Rachel Kramer Bussel

Irresistible features loving couples who turn their deepest fantasies into reality—resulting in uninhibited, imaginative sex they can only enjoy together.
ISBN 978-1-57344-762-1 $14.95

Sweet Confessions
Erotic Fantasies for Couples
Edited by Violet Blue

In *Sweet Confessions*, Violet Blue showcases inspirational "you can do it, too" tales that are perfect bedtime reading for lovers. The lust-inciting fantasies include spanking, exhibitionism, role-playing, three-ways and sensual adventures that will embolden real couples to reach new heights of passion.
ISBN 978-1-57344-665-5 $14.95

Ordering is easy! Call us toll free or fax us to place your MC/VISA order.
You can also mail the order form below with payment to:
Cleis Press, 2246 Sixth St., Berkeley, CA 94710.

**Buy 4 books,
Get 1 FREE***

ORDER FORM

QTY	TITLE	PRICE

SUBTOTAL _____

SHIPPING _____

SALES TAX _____

TOTAL _____

Add $3.95 postage/handling for the first book ordered and $1.00 for each additional book. Outside North America, please contact us for shipping rates. California residents add 9% sales tax. Payment in U.S. dollars only.

* Free book of equal or lesser value. Shipping and applicable sales tax extra.

Cleis Press • Phone: (800) 780-2279 • Fax: (510) 845-8001
orders@cleispress.com • www.cleispress.com
You'll find more great books on our website

Follow us on Twitter @cleispress • Friend/fan us on Facebook